Hush, Dear Sister
Audra McElyea

Counterplay Press

Copyright © [2024] by [Audra McElyea]

AudraMcElyea.com

All rights reserved.

No portion of this book may be reproduced in any form without written permission from the publisher or author, except as permitted by U.S. copyright law.

This is a work of fiction. Names, characters, places, and incidents either are the product of the author's imagination or are used fictitiously, and any resemblance to locales, events, business establishments, or actual persons, living or dead, is entirely coincidental.

www.CounterplayPress.com

Contents

Dedication		VII
1.	Chapter 1	1
2.	Chapter 2	15
3.	Chapter 3	32
4.	Chapter 4	43
5.	Chapter 5	58
6.	Chapter 6	67
7.	Chapter 7	81
8.	Chapter 8	95
9.	Chapter 9	108
10.	Chapter 10	123
11.	Chapter 11	133
12.	Chapter 12	143
13.	Chapter 13	156
14.	Chapter 14	164
15.	Chapter 15	175

16.	Chapter 16	189
17.	Chapter 17	199
18.	Chapter 18	207
19.	Chapter 19	216
20.	Chapter 20	224
21.	Chapter 21	234
22.	Chapter 22	244
23.	Chapter 23	252
24.	Chapter 24	259
25.	Chapter 25	267
Acknowledgements		274
About the author		277
Also by Audra McElyea		279
Also by Audra McElyea		282

For my sister, Laura. Thank God we aren't like these broads.

Chapter 1

Rain pours on the sidewalk, creating an eerie mist as a terrified woman stops in front of a sinister, but beautiful, gothic revival mansion. Her panic draws me into the scene as she continues to distance herself from a man emerging from the woods behind her with a knife. And even though I know how it all ends, I continue to play with the ends of my hair like I've never seen it before.

Her on-screen appeal is almost tangible—the perfect combination of girl-next-door and tortured, scary-movie soul. And she looks nothing like I do now. I glance down at my still swollen right leg, marked with fresh scars underneath a bulky brace, and wonder if it'll ever look the way it once did.

Monroe tucks my legs in under the fleece blanket, turns to find the remote on my nightstand, and raises the volume of *The Night I Died*. But when she sets out a bowl of popcorn between us, I'm redirected even more to the present, to my real life, and I no longer feel the distracting tension playing out on TV.

I rub the back of my neck and close my eyes before taking a good look around, barely able to stomach the sight of my current life compared to what it was. So much has changed in the last month alone, much less since filming this movie.

The opening credits and title flash across the TV screen, and the movie now shows a thunderstorm brewing as my character slips and almost falls on the front porch. Monroe looks at me with child-like excitement when my character enters the unlocked house, wet and trembling as she clings to the door frame for support.

I can tell by the huge grin on Monroe's face that she thinks this is one of the best ideas she's ever had. For some odd reason she thinks I'll enjoy this, that it'll motivate me or be good for my healing. But she's wrong.

Monroe shoves another piece of popcorn into her mouth and pulls her platinum hair into a perfect messy bun at the nape of her neck as she cuddles closer to me and talks with her mouth full. "This is my favorite part. I love how you and Matthew ad-libbed your lines after you barged in his house. It was genius."

"We were a good team, but Crawford Manor was the star," I say with a soft smile as I look around the 120-year-old master bedroom I've known and loved since starring in *The Night I Died* fifteen years ago.

I fell so deeply in love with the home's grandeur and darkness during filming that I bought it from the owner as soon as the movie wrapped, and I've never regretted it.

Back then, a lot of people found the estate creepy and thought it was haunted, but having been a part of the film that gave it that reputation, I knew better. Of course, there were rumors of hauntings going into filming, and that's why the producers chose it to begin with, but insiders knew none of the stories were actually true.

I fell in love with its pitched gables, stained-glass arched windows, thirteen-foot ceilings, secret staircases, and ornate moldings and trimmings, but most of all I fell in love with the memories it housed. Memories of the best time of my life. When I first met Charlie. But it also holds something I want to stay hidden, a truth no one else knows about that happened here in this house. A dark secret I've held onto for many years.

A TV host appears during the movie's intermission while Monroe runs to the bathroom. I hang my head when I see the headline on the bottom of the screen reading *Annette Taylor Update*, thinking this is how people will always think of me from now on.

"It's been one month since actress Annette Taylor's tragic home invasion left her with a broken femur in one leg, a sprained ankle in the other, and permanent nerve damage to her thigh after the surgery. After her neighbor was also robbed last week, police caught and arrested Thomas Nichols who admitted to both break-ins but said Ms. Taylor had been injured prior to his arrival. TikTok fans are already speculating that—"

The host is quickly cut off when Monroe hurries into my room and mutes the TV. She changes the subject to food until the movie comes back on, but I can't help thinking about the man's face they flashed on the screen and what really happened that night.

Is he really the one who did this to me, or is he telling the truth? Knowing there's even a slight possibility he's being honest terrifies me, because that means whoever really did this is still out there. And who's to say they won't come back again to finish me off.

"This film is a masterpiece. Our great-grandchildren will watch it years from now, and it'll still hold up." Monroe fixes her gaze on the TV as the credits roll.

But before I can point out that she's also starred in many epic films herself, another breaking news headline flashes across the bottom of the screen as a different news anchor appears with a grim expression.

"Kelly Logan here with a shocking news headline. Fans were dismayed this evening when actress Vera Green fainted and appeared to have a seizure live on the red carpet at the premiere of her new film in downtown Los Angeles. We are now sorry to report she passed away in the ambulance on her way to the hospital. Police are investigating what happened, and we'll know more on this story as information comes in."

Monroe and I both look at each other with raised brows as we grab our phones to make sure this report is accurate.

The woman continues, "However, fans are already speculating and pointing out that she had the mysterious, seizure-like reaction right after drinking water during her red-carpet interview. But for now, our thoughts are with Vera's family and friends during this tragic time. Vera was only twenty-nine years old and was just nominated for her second Oscar in the Best Actress category. There is no doubt she will truly be missed by many."

Monroe mutes the TV and stares at me before we both scroll through various news sources on our phones that have similar headlines.

"What the hell?" she says as she reads.

"Oh my God. This can't be real, can it?" I see post after post of videos on Twitter showing Vera shaking and foaming at the mouth on the red-carpet floor. "This is awful. God, I can't watch this." I clutch my stomach, kill the app, then set down my phone.

"I haven't heard that she was into anything illicit," Monroe adds as she types on her phone and winces.

I haven't heard either, but the speculation's already out there on the internet. Even if she did struggle with addiction, I can't imagine how horrible it is for her family to see her dying on social media with people just standing there taking pictures and videos.

Vera and I never crossed paths, but everyone loved her. She was young, beautiful, and insanely talented. No matter why she collapsed on the red carpet, it's a deep loss for the film community.

"Maybe she had a medical condition and the stress of the premiere got to her or something," I speculate as I play with my hair, trying to convince myself that we aren't all just a few seconds away from tragically dropping dead.

Since my accident, I've felt this continual sense of impending doom. Like I'm waiting for another major tragedy to run my life off the rails even further, proving that what happened to me last month was only the beginning.

After my parents' sudden death one year ago and my incident last month, Vera's sketchy death on the red carpet makes it feel like there's some kind of curse all around me.

I can't hear a word Monroe is saying about Vera's latest film because I'm lost in my own paralyzing daze of intrusive thoughts, but when the sound of my sister's car pulling into my driveway registers in my mind, it causes chills of anxiety to go up and down my arms.

Monroe and I both look at each other with darting eyes before she makes a swift move to know for certain. She leaps off the bed, rushes to the floor-length window in the corner of my bedroom, and peers toward the concrete pavers with a knowing sigh of dread.

If I didn't already know from Monroe's look of disgust that it is, in fact, Sophia pulling up, I'd know it now. The distinct slam of her car door and the sound of her voice yelling at someone give her away at once. Only I can't tell if she's screaming with excitement or anger, and I silently pray it's not the latter.

I love my sister, but she *is* known for her moodiness—and, like me, she's really been hurting since our parents' unexpected deaths last year.

"You know you can always come stay with me. She keeps you too isolated here. Plus, she's batshit crazy, and it's not good for you." Monroe shakes her head with disapproval and moves away from the window.

"And if you ask me, she's only willing to help because you're more famous and have this big estate. Otherwise you'd be left in the dust to figure things out for yourself, and you know it."

Monroe plops back down on the bed and pleads with me yet again, her emerald eyes full of worry, to get away from my sister as I tightly grip my blanket with my fists. She and Sophia have always despised one another, and no matter what happens, I don't see that ever changing.

Monroe's always been good to me, and I love her like a sister, but she does tend to rub some people the wrong way with her brutal honesty. There was a time in our twenties when Monroe said something in an interview about Sophia that she shouldn't have, and though Monroe eventually apologized, I can't help but still feel terrible for how badly Sophia was humiliated by it.

Monroe still tends to tell it like it is, and some people never get past that quality to see her big heart. To say Sophia still holds a grudge against her for what she did is probably the understatement of the century.

"She's trying," I tell Monroe, attempting to keep the peace between them. "She's doing her best."

And it isn't untrue. Sophia got a chair-lift system installed so I can go upstairs if I want. Is the system old? Yes. And I can't work it alone yet because I can't transfer from the wheelchair to the lift chair and back to the wheelchair again without help, but it works—and it's the thought of independence I like about it anyway.

"Besides, there's no way you can keep caring for me once filming picks up again. And maybe it'd be good for my sister and me to be together."

Monroe makes a face. There's nothing I can really say that will make her forgive my sister, or make Sophia forgive Monroe. Sophia has issues to work through for sure, and maybe all this time together will allow us to work through them. Sister to sister, face to face.

"You're acting like you're a burden, when really you're a saint for letting her stay with you after all she's done," Monroe mutters. "She's a bitter—"

"Enough," I say rather sharply. Everyone knows my sister's career tanked and mine didn't, and maybe Sophia is a little bitter about that, but I'd be a little bitter, too, if our roles were reversed.

Monroe shuts my door and locks it from the inside.

I wince. "She's not going to like that."

"She doesn't like anything." Monroe rolls her eyes.

That isn't necessarily true. Sophia likes being nice to people who can help her career. That counts, doesn't it? And I think in some weird way Sophia loves me, despite all we've been through together and individually. I'd bet my life on it.

"I don't care what she doesn't like. This is your house, and you don't need to feel controlled or contained by her. And I'm not the only one who thinks you need to give her the boot and hire a full-time nurse or doctor or something. Charlie told me he thinks ..." Monroe starts, but I interrupt her before she can finish.

"No. I just, I just can't. Can we please not talk about Charlie again?"

I drag my injured legs over toward the edge of the bed by lifting and sliding them with my braced arms and reach for my glass of water on the nightstand.

"I just don't have it in me today." I take a long sip.

Footsteps in the kitchen echo through the foyer and travel toward my room.

"Fine." Monroe gives in and reaches for the knob to unlock it. "But he still loves you, just so you know. And for the record, I think you're making a big mistake."

The doorknob clicks just as Sophia's hurried footsteps approach my door, and my chest tightens with every echoed step she takes as I try my best to mentally prepare myself for Sophia and Monroe being in the same room.

"Annette! Annette!" Sophia screams with a kind of genuine excitement I haven't heard from her in a long time.

Monroe opens the door just as she arrives, and Sophia barges in out of breath.

"You're never going to believe it. You're just not!" Sophia cries with a huge grin on her face.

"What? What is it?" I perk up on the bed as much as my body will allow.

"We just heard about Vera Green if that's what you're talking about," Monroe says, and I hope to God that's not why Sophia's smiling.

Sophia turns to Monroe for a quick nod of acknowledgement, then subtly flips her long, dark brown hair behind her shoulder before she continues.

"No, I mean, I saw that, and God it was dreadful, but no ... something else. Remember how I pitched my own reality show to Frank Baxter years ago and he acted like a complete dick and never even called me back?"

I wince as Monroe rolls her eyes behind Sophia's back. "Yeah. I remember. Maybe he was just busy or ..."

"Whatever"—Sophia talks over me—"it doesn't matter. So ... Frank just called me because he caught *The Night I Died* on TV today, and it reminded him of my pitch. Anyway, he calls me up and says he wants to film a documentary of our life together following your accident. He thinks it'd be a huge hit since people are looking for more diversity on TV now. And, I mean, with you being crippled or whatever, we would be a great fit."

My face grows warm with embarrassment at the insensitive way Sophia speaks of my current condition, and I can only pray Monroe is able to contain herself from flying off the handle at Sophia's crude remark.

"Oh," I say, feeling stunned and unable to completely process everything she just said. "Well, what did you say to Frank?" I ask, being careful not to commit to doing the show. The last thing on Earth I want to do right now is have the entire world see me like *this*.

Monroe's jaw clenches, and she spews her own response before Sophia can answer. "She's not crippled! And normal people don't talk that way, Sophia."

Sophia turns toward Monroe with raised brows. "Disabled, then." She waves her hand as if it were a small technicality.

Monroe steps toward Sophia, and she takes a step back. "Annette is going to walk again ... I don't care what the doctor says about nerve damage. All we know for sure is that she's injured temporarily. And please, for the love of God, don't refer to her or anyone else as *crippled* ever again."

"Of course, she'll walk again." Sophia smiles my way with a head tilt.

"It's just, these days you just never know what words to use for stuff, and God knows people are so damn sensitive." She gently takes a seat on the edge of my bed with her hands perfectly clasped in her lap.

If you didn't know her, you'd think her a proper lady with her perfect posture and look of adoration toward her only sister. A look that really means she needs something from me, something I won't want to give her.

She places a hand on my right leg and lightly rubs it. "Annette, don't you think a TV show is just what we need? I mean, it's perfect: two sisters who are both famous actresses, living together under one roof while facing their own adversities. The people of America want us in their lives right now, so let's give it to them."

I grab the pillow beside me and hold it to my chest as she continues to try and convince me to be on a glorified reality show with her even though we've not spoken for the better part of fifteen years until recently.

"It can help us be able to afford the very best of care for you. Maybe we can even hire Doctor Lang to come here full-time and care for you until you recover!" She rubs her hands together.

"You wouldn't even need to leave the house for appointments anymore. Wouldn't that be ideal? No more entering back doors at the doctors anymore to avoid the paps."

I take a deep breath and consider the validity of the points she's made as my stomach turns equally with the fear of saying yes and with the repercussions of telling Sophia no.

But how can I possibly be expected to share my mess of a life with the public? It'll only taint the successful acting career I've worked so hard to achieve over the years. But at the same time,

I wonder how I can afford to turn an offer like this down when money is already tight.

After all the times I've given my parents and Sophia money for her rehab and the unexpected costs associated with Mom and Dad's funeral, I'm not exactly sitting pretty, and the last thing I want is to lose my house on top of everything else.

I mean, it's not like I can get work in movies right now. I'm hopeful for the future, but who knows if my leg will ever be the same or what that'll mean for acting roles. And even with all that pushed aside, I'm not a spring chicken anymore, and we all know Hollywood likes them young and fresh.

Monroe shrugs my way like Sophia has a point. "It's up to you, Annette. If it's something you can get on board with and be excited about, maybe it would help with your depression. Give you something to do every day, for now. And private home health care from a doctor you already trust *would* be amazing. But it's a *lot* to ask."

She narrows her eyes toward Sophia, who is clearly champing at the bit for me to say yes with her bejeweled hands tightly fisted together. I recognize two of the many rings adorning her fingers as antique cocktail rings Mom left to her and wish she was here with me right now.

I look out the window at the changing leaves and picture the secret I know I have with this house and how much it means to me to keep it. As a red leaf cascades from its branch, I picture Sophia's dark past resurfacing on the show, on full display for a brand-new generation to see, criticize, and discuss on social media.

What would be worse ... being haunted by the demons of the past again, or being haunted with regret in the future for turning down this window of opportunity after I lose everything?

"Have Frank come over, and we can at least discuss it," I finally say, and Sophia releases her clasped hands and gives me a huge smile full of relief. Only just as she does, I can't help but notice a single drop of blood rolling down her wrist.

As she rises from my bed, I hold my breath as it slides off her porcelain skin and down her pinky finger. It splashes onto my white duvet in slow-motion with a deafening reminder of just how intense Sophia can be, and of what might happen if she knew my secret.

"I'll go call him now," Sophia says as she reaches the threshold, seemingly unaware of the troubling bloodstain she's left behind.

Chapter 2

Three days later, at two o'clock in the afternoon, Sophia barges into my room with freshly curled hair and a face full of makeup as I'm watching the news from my bed. My right ankle is twice its normal size after I tested the waters and put weight on it this morning. I know I need more time to heal from my infection before I can do any kind of physical therapy, but being this helpless and immobile is really starting to drive me insane.

The woman reading the news says she has an update on Vera Green's death, and Sophia and I both hold our breath as we listen.

"Police have confirmed that Vera Green was poisoned. They've asked for anyone with videos or photos from last night's red-carpet event that shows anyone handling the water bottle Vera drank from, besides her assistant Vinny Parker, to share it with authorities by calling this number. The chief of police says this is now an ongoing murder investigation and should be taken very seriously by everyone."

I cover my mouth with my hands. "She was murdered?"

After my attack last month, there are a lot of fans on TikTok who are questioning whether someone could be targeting actresses, and they're already calling them the Red-Carpet Killer. No one knows anything for sure, except since Thomas Nichols is still in jail, it couldn't have been him. And even though their conspiracy theories are unlikely, I can't help feeling unsafe if there really is a serial killer in town with a specific vendetta against actresses.

Sophia sighs and shakes her head with disbelief. "This is crazy."

Then she clears her throat and seemingly tries to change the subject before I notice she looks scared. "Well, it's a good thing we'll have cameras watching our backs soon, huh?"

I stare blankly at the TV then turn it off, wondering if meeting with Frank is the right thing to do.

"Frank's on his way now, so let's do something with that hair of yours—fix you up a little." Sophia aggressively brushes my light brown hair into a high bun and digs bobby pins into my dirty scalp with a snarled nose.

Holding back my tears about Vera, I can't help but feel like Sophia's trying to distract me from the massive problem in front of us. If any of the crazy theories are true, us putting ourselves out there as two actresses on this reality show could be inadvertently setting ourselves up to be the killer's next victims.

"Let's do some dry shampoo." She runs to my bathroom to grab a fresh can as I wait on my bed and muster up the bravery to ask her to help me wash my hair again. Feeling this sore and weak a month after the accident still baffles me, and I can see why Sophia gets frustrated with my glacial progress sometimes.

"Sorry, it's been since Monroe was here that it's been washed. Do you think you could help me shower tonight?" I wince and pick at my nails as I wait for her response, glad that I can't see her facial expressions.

Helping me maneuver into the shower and bathe is probably Sophia's least favorite thing to assist me with because it requires so much effort and heavy lifting, plus she always ends up getting wet in the end as well. But it's no picnic for me either, being naked and vulnerable in front of my judgmental sister who always comments that I stink.

Sophia returns with a can of heavily scented dry shampoo and a bottle of perfume. "Now, if you can get into your wheelchair and get yourself to the bathroom, then you can certainly get yourself in the shower and do your business. It'll be good for you to figure it out and build up some stamina."

I blink back tears knowing she just politely told me no as she sprays me down like a dirty dog, and I fan my face with my hands, still choking on the fumes.

"Oh, it's not that bad, you drama queen. Just hold your breath a minute for God's sake," Sophia says with a menacing chuckle as I squeeze the blanket on my lap with my hand.

I know she's trying to push me out of my depression by not coddling or enabling me, but right now all she's doing is discouraging me further and making me feel like a huge burden.

I cough one last time and hold my breath as the buzzer for the front gate goes off with a loud echo.

"I'll go let him in. Be back in a few minutes." Sophia scurries down toward the hallway.

"Let me work some magic with him alone first. I'll come get you when I'm ready." She stops to gaze at her reflection in the hallway mirror, then pinches her cheeks.

I finally inhale again once she leaves then gag at the potency of the coverup she left behind. My head throbs as the fog continues to enter my nostrils, and I wonder if Frank can smell me all the way from the gate.

A few seconds later, I hear the front door creak open as my sister's friendliest voice echoes all the way to my bedroom. It's the particular high tone of voice she specifically reserves for those she can gain the most out of, and I can't help but sigh with exasperation at her predictability.

She always was one to charm her way into just about anything she wanted, even as a kid. After fixing my face, I yawn more than should be humanly possible for ten ... twenty ... then thirty minutes as they laugh and chat without me before Sophia finally makes her way back to my room. It honestly reminds me of the *hurry up and wait* you experience on film sets after you've spent three hours getting your makeup done only for there to be a timely holdup with production.

"He's ready." Sophia bursts into my bedroom with a happy dance, pleased to see that I've managed to get myself into my wheelchair and then into the bathroom where I finished my makeup.

"I think I've talked him into a million for twelve episodes for the two of us to split. Of course, anyone else that appears as a 'friend' will get compensated as well on top of that figure, given they sign all the waivers, that is." She talks a mile a minute before she stops to look in my antique vanity mirror where she fluffs her long, dark hair.

"I'm ready when you are," I say as she continues to mouth words and smile at herself in the mirror. When I speak, she abruptly drops her arms and turns back around to look at me with an annoyed expression, as if she'd already forgotten I was there.

"Fine." She forces a smile as she grabs the bedroom door and opens it for me, and it's then that I wonder if she resents that we have to share the limelight of this show in order for it to work.

When I wheel down the hall and into the foyer, I spy Frank Baxter on my white leather sofa in the living room. Bald head, arms spread out on the back of the couch, and legs spread out in a relaxed position as he turns and smiles with that notorious gap in between his two front teeth showing.

"Well, my oh my, there she is. Just as beautiful as ever with her megawatt smile," he says in his slow, Texas drawl as he stands then meets me for a kiss on the hand as my heart races into my throat.

"Nice to see you again, Frank." I force a smile, feeling embarrassed to be seen in this rough condition while wondering what he really thinks seeing me this way for the first time.

"What have you two cooked up so far?" I wipe my sweaty palms on my pants, not wanting to feel pressure to speak next. I need to try and calm my nerves and act normal—even if I feel like my condition is a huge elephant in the room right now.

Despite Sophia's efforts to fix my hair and mine to apply makeup, I look thin, pale, and like I've been run over by a truck and taped back together. I have a huge bruise on my cheek and under each eye, my arms and legs are still black and blue, my neck is still stiff and sore, my ankle is huge, and my thigh is hidden underneath a ginormous brace that thankfully masks its mutiny after they not-so-successfully repaired it with a rod.

But what Frank can't see is how much more damage has been done to me on the inside. I'm depressed and heartbroken, and I don't know if I'll ever truly recover from all my trauma.

Frank takes a seat back on the couch with Sophia as I wheel over beside them. "Well, like I told Sophia, don't think of this as a reality show. Think of it as a real-life, twelve-episode, gritty, but live, documentary of your life after the accident that shows how you're healing."

Sophia chimes in, "Frank says people are enamored with your story right now and want to know more."

My eyes widen with surprise and concern as I take in one specific word Frank just said. "Wait. Frank, did you say *live* show?"

Frank clears his throat. "Well, we worked out that it can be filmed via cameras set up in your house. It won't stream live, but we'll gather organic footage at all times. That is unless you're in a room and specifically turn that camera off for a period of time for some privacy."

I furrow my brows. "So we can turn them off whenever we want?"

"Technically, yes. But what's going to make this documentary a success is the realness, so I would encourage you to not turn any of the cameras off unless you really feel like you need to. Does that make sense?" Frank asks hardly blinking.

His unique intensity has always been off-the-charts quirky and charismatic from as far back as I can remember. I often used to wonder why such a complex character was behind the camera rather than in front of it.

"Yeah, it makes sense. So there won't be a crew here at all, then?" I tilt my head, forgetting for a second how sore my neck still is. And I have to admit, not having a camera crew in my face all the time does make this sound a hell of a lot more appealing.

"No crew in sight. Nobody will be here in Gray Woods, California, but you two. But we will have producers watching the live feed just around the corner in L.A. They'll be on duty around the clock reviewing footage they think we should throw into the episodes." Frank winks as Sophia nods along unable to sit still.

"So, if there is a serial killer out there after actresses, you two are safe and secure with all these cameras filming you," he chuckles, and I find myself picking at my nails.

"Well, surely Vera's incident and mine had nothing to do with each other. That's just ridiculous." I feel a pit of concern in my stomach. It's way too far-fetched, even by Hollywood's standards. Isn't it?

After another hour of ironing out potential pitfalls and other details surrounding filming, Frank heads toward the front door with an excited look on his face as Sophia and I digest everything. "Grace Wallace still your agent?"

"She is." I grin, knowing he's tried to get her to hook up with him for the past twenty years despite failing miserably.

"Fifty-something years old now, and she's still a smoking-hot ball-buster." He shakes his head. "I look forward to sending the contract over to her."

A day later, I doze off uncharacteristically after lunch on my living room couch. I suddenly find myself slumped on my left side with drool oozing out of my mouth as something shakes my shoulders with purpose.

"Yes, I'd be willing to be on camera. I'm slowly transitioning into high-profile house calls like this full-time now anyway. Annette can swing the cost, right?" I hear a familiar man's voice ask with a British accent.

"For heaven's sake, Annette, wake up." I'm jostled by my shoulders once again by Sophia. "Doctor Lang is here to talk about home care."

I lift my groggy head up as the room spins a little. "Doctor Lang's here? Why didn't you wake me up earlier?"

Sophia helps me into a seated position, my body clad in sweats. Before lunch, Sophia was also in loungewear, but now she's in a perfect-for-fall-time maxi dress with her hair done and makeup on while I look like I belong on the streets.

"Thanks for coming all the way out here, Doctor Lang." I try to calm my disheveled hair and place a blanket over my spot of drool on the couch. Sophia looks at me with wide eyes, then gives Dr. Lang a longing glance as she motions for him to have a seat.

"I'm sorry, I don't know what happened. I must've conked out after lunch, I guess," I try to explain as I feel my entire face grow warm and tingly.

Despite the fact Dr. Lang was our parents' friend and is at least fifteen years older than us, Sophia's always tried, and failed, to flirt with him. Maybe it's because he knows her troubling history, or because he was so close to our mom and dad, but he's never reciprocated any interest despite her efforts, and I doubt he ever will.

But now that Sophia and I are over forty and Dr. Lang's been divorced for many years, it seems to me like maybe she's going to try her luck again anyway. I mean, I get it; he's got salt-and-pepper hair, a trim but fit build, and a swoon-worthy English accent. What's not to like?

"No problem. I told Sophia I'd come by and check on you since you're considering me for home care. We discussed that I'd still be working at the office as well, but I'll be able to carve out some time to come here regularly if you ladies decide to go in that direction." He pats me on the back.

Sophia takes a seat across from me and beams at Dr. Lang as he continues, "You two are like family to me, after all. And no, Sophia, I don't mind being filmed for your documentary, as long as it's only for medical purposes," he adds, standing tall next to me.

"Tell her what you said about the show and work being good for her depression." Sophia uncrosses her legs and plays with her hair.

"Oh, yes. I do think having daily work would be good for your mental health. Maybe we can start to lower your depression medication if I start to see an improvement. Work will be a good distraction. If you're on board with the idea, that is."

I pick at my unkempt fingernails and second guess what I've signed myself up for. "I think I am. I just need to speak with my agent first. You know, before I sign anything." I sigh knowing Grace is probably going to think I've gone crazy for even thinking about doing this.

But they're not wrong. I do think some consistency would make a difference in my mental state. The ever-changing nurses who all ask the same questions every day make it impossible to feel like anyone really knows what's going on with me. And even though I can't even try putting weight on my leg again for eight more weeks or go to physical therapy yet because of my infection, it'd be helpful to have someone following my progress who can encourage me. Even if the only improvement is that my bruises are finally becoming less noticeable.

Dr. Lang studies me with a serious expression and takes a seat next to me on the couch. "Well, hopefully you'll find being seen and heard at this time in your life can help inspire others who look up to you as well. And perhaps you'll enjoy the show in the end."

His phone buzzes a few times, and he stands to leave. "Plus, I know your parents would be proud that you two girls are in this together ... as a team," he adds as he gathers his things.

I look toward Sophia who has her hands pointed toward Dr. Lang in the prayer position with a soft smile and agree. "Yeah. I bet they would."

"You need to have some sort of creative license on this. I suggested you add it into your contract to approve of and sign off on all final footage after it's spliced together for each episode, because you don't want to come off to the public as being in worse health than you actually are—especially mentally," Grace explains after she speaks with Frank about my contract.

And she's right. That kind of negativity irreparably kills careers and people's self-esteem. That's why everyone needs a good agent who has their back in ways they hadn't even thought about yet. After all, the devil is in the details.

Grace clears her throat then sighs. "Plus, I don't want your sister to have any kind of creative control of the show. She could create a negative edit for you, and with you-all's history, I wouldn't put it past her to try and undermine you in some way."

I take a deep breath knowing Grace despises Sophia just as much as Monroe does. "I hear you. But Sophia and I are in a very different place now than we were in our twenties when you met her." I wish Grace could see how different Sophia's been lately. I mean, I can hardly believe it's the same person myself. She's really changed for the better since my accident, and while I get Grace's *better safe than sorry* mentality as my agent, I don't really think it's necessary.

"Did Frank go for that amendment?" I ask, even though I'm pretty sure I already know the answer.

"He went for it by the time I got through with him, as well as a two-hundred-thousand-dollar signing bonus, since *you're* the one drawing in viewers, and fifty thousand dollars for home repairs you may need to do after filming begins." She smiles with pride I can practically hear through the phone.

"I'll email you the new contract when he approves it, but I just wanted to check in and hear your voice myself," she says, sounding skeptical that I'd even consider doing a show like this, much less with my sister.

Sophia needs the industry to give her another chance, and I can't help thinking that if I can give her that, certainly others will be able to as well. It's ironic that an industry who makes so many films about second chances is so unwilling to practice what they preach.

"I'm here for you if you need anything, and I think this can be good for you as long as you don't let your sister take over or make the show into a train-wreck with her drinking."

"I-I don't think that will be a problem. She's been living with me for a month now, and I haven't seen any signs of her falling off the wagon or anything."

Grace takes a deep breath, seemingly contemplating what she's going to say next with care. "I know you love her and want to see the best in her, but it needs to be said ... Watch your back. I'm glad that doctor will be checking in on you personally now. It makes me feel better about you being stuck in that house alone with her all the time."

Grace has always been a constant voice of reason for me in the past, but I think she's wrong about my sister. "You're sweet to worry, and I promise I'll let you know if anything changes," I finally say, trying to firmly cement my stance on continuing to talk about my sister.

Grace clears her throat, and I can hear another phone ringing in the background at her office. "Okay. Sounds good. As for the show itself goes, try to keep it very real and documentary-like, and if you ever want me to look over the footage, I'd be glad to help you make judgment calls on edits."

Sophia calls out to me from the kitchen, "I'm going to the store. Be back in thirty."

"Okay," I yell back as I cover the bottom of my phone with my hand. Then she slams the door going out into the driveway, not because she's angry, but because the word *gentle* isn't in her vocabulary.

"Okay, Grace. Thanks so much. I may end up taking you up on reviewing the episodes at some point." And we both hang up with a sense of awkwardness between us.

I flip on the TV in my room, but after skimming through Netflix for thirty minutes, I ultimately decide I'm too mentally exhausted from scrolling titles to watch any. So I turn the TV off, lie down, and shut my now burning eyes.

Only as soon as I do, I swear I hear the floorboards creaking upstairs. My eyes widen, and I feel more awake as I lean over my bed and peer out the window for Sophia's car, hoping it was her somehow even though I know there's no way she'd be back this soon.

Orange and red leaves descend from the oak tree onto a carless driveway, telling me she's not back yet, so I decide the noises must have been the wind or the house settling. But I turn the TV back on for background noise just in case. I try to distract myself by grabbing my phone so I can check my email for the new contract Grace was supposed to send.

Contract attached below. Also, I didn't want to say this on the phone because I thought you may get upset with me, but have you considered calling Charlie and taking him up on his offer to take care of you? That way you wouldn't feel like you HAVE to do this show. I know you all broke up right before the accident, but everyone knows you two were something special... Just think about it

.

I slam my phone down on my nightstand, mute the TV, and curl into a sleeping position again the best I can. Only this time, I hear low voices murmuring somewhere upstairs. Adrenaline shoots through my body, and I sit straight up in my bed with rapid breaths, knowing I'm dead if the Red-Carpet Killer's here.

With quivering arms, I scoot toward the edge of the bed. Do I get in my wheelchair and try to make it to old man Godfrey's house next door, or do I try to hide under my bed? I decide on the latter, knowing that old man Godfrey's house would take an eternity to reach in my wheelchair, being almost a quarter of a mile away.

With sweaty palms, I grab my phone then try to lower myself onto my wheelchair, only it's not locked into place. With too much momentum, I overshoot and tumble to the floor instead with a loud thud on my right shoulder and hip, giving my location away. After my already battered body hits the hardwood floor, I gasp in pain and wince at the extra noise I just made.

I hold my breath and don't move another muscle even though my shoulder is throbbing and my heart is racing. Not only did I drop my phone when I fell, but it slid about six feet away from me. The voices upstairs grow quiet as I lie still, but the creaking of the floorboards above me begins again.

I scoot-crawl over to my phone, then back under the bed with all the strength I can muster and dial 911. My shaking hand hovers over the send button, and I go back and forth about whether I should complete the call. This is going to be so embarrassing if Sophia simply left a TV on upstairs or something and that's all I heard.

But no, I am certain I know the difference between real voices and people speaking through a TV. And a TV couldn't make the floorboards creak. So I reluctantly decide to hit send. The dispatcher on the other end of the line asks for my emergency in a voice so calm it makes me want to panic and shout so she feels my urgency.

But I whisper back to her instead. "I think there's someone in my house. I was robbed about a month ago, and I think they're back. I hear voices and noises upstairs. I'm badly injured already, and I'm all alone in the house." Then I answer all of her questions about any potential weapons and exit strategies as I tremble under my bed.

"We're sending an officer who is already close to your house right now. Just stay on the line with me until they arrive, Ms. Taylor. Okay? In your condition, I think it's best to stay put and wait for help," she says in an assuring voice that only makes me sound crazier as I speak to her through frightened tears.

"Can you take a few deep breaths for me, Annette?" she finally asks when I sound like I'm going to hyperventilate.

Hearing myself breathe heavily as my heart threatens to burst out of my chest isn't helping my anxiety, but I do find it weird that the only other person on my mind right now is Charlie. He's the only one I want here to protect me in this insane moment ... he's the only one I miss.

After being trapped under my bed for what seems like an hour, but is probably only a few short minutes, I hear a car pull in the driveway. A car door slams shut, and I take some deep breaths and close my eyes, finally feeling some relief.

"Help is here!" I say to the lady as the phone slips from my sweaty palm and I accidentally hit end.

Chapter 3

"I'm back. Got you some of those gluten-free cookies you love," Sophia yells as she enters the kitchen from the driveway, and I start to panic all over again thinking she should be quiet in case someone is waiting to attack her.

I really thought it was the police who'd arrived. And damnit, why did I have to hit end on my phone? What if TikTok was right and there is some lunatic Red-Carpet Killer out there? Only they aren't *out there*, they're in here.

Sophia's shuffling footsteps make their way from the kitchen into the foyer with no hesitation or concern as I cover my mouth with my hands. But even though she deserves a warning, I can't let myself scream out—it will only draw more attention to both of us, and she's probably heading toward my room to check on me anyway.

My bedroom door creaks open just as my pulse races all the way up into my already tight throat. Then, from underneath my bed, I see her feet turn in a circle of confusion before she finally says, "Annette? Where the hell are you?"

"I'm here," I whisper with a shaky voice I don't even recognize. "Someone's here. Upstairs or in the attic. I called the police, and they're on their way."

Sophia gets down on her hands and knees, eyes me under the bed, and giggles. "You're pulling my leg, aren't you? Get out from under there, you goof!"

I shush her with my quivering hands and whisper, "I heard voices upstairs. For real, someone's here. Maybe two people."

"No, there's not." She smiles at me like I'm a child playing a game of hide-and-seek.

"Now get out from under there before you hurt yourself." She grabs my arms and drags me out roughly like I'm a doll, then leaves me on the floor beside the bed.

"This isn't funny. Do you have any idea how hard it's going to be for me to get you back up in your bed now?" She huffs and puffs with frustration as she rolls her sleeves up, refusing to take me seriously.

"No, Sophia, someone's up there. Maybe the fans are right and someone did this to me, then killed Vera," I whisper again, even though she's making enough noise to wake the dead. "I'm telling you ... I heard voices and footsteps."

Sophia lifts me back into my wheelchair with all her strength, lowers the arm on one side, then pushes me onto the bed with an exasperated grunt. "Doctor Lang said your depression and anxiety may get worse, and if it does, then I need to up your dosages. And if you're seriously hearing voices, then we've got even bigger problems than depression. I'm going to go upstairs and check just to prove it to you."

"Sophia, no! The police will be here any minute. Let them go with you," I beg. "Or at least take a weapon with you just in case. Maybe a kitchen knife or something."

Sophia rolls her eyes. "Fine, I'll grab my revolver out of my room if it makes you feel better."

"You have a revolver?" I ask, not sure whether I'm grateful or terrified.

"Yes, I have a revolver," she says in a high-pitched voice, as though everyone else in the world has one besides me.

"Well, be careful, and lock my door when you leave." I pull the covers up to my chin because I'm somehow sweating and shivering at the same time.

Sophia walks over to my bedroom door, *doesn't* click the knob to lock it, and shuts it behind her. "I promise, you'll be fine," she says with confidence from the other side.

She shuffles to the foyer, up the grand staircase to the guest bedroom she's been staying in, and opens a squeaky drawer before making her way up the next set of stairs into the attic, shouting, "Ready or not, here I come."

I wince at the thought of her being so flippant in her search and wait with my phone quivering in my hands, feeling helpless. Time seems to go by in slow motion as I wait for something terrible to happen to her, but then I hear another car pull in the driveway and a car door shuts. The police are here.

Sophia must've left the kitchen door unlocked because an officer announces his presence as he comes into the house. It's then that I wonder how he got past the iron gate outside …

"This is the police. I have my weapon drawn. Annette Taylor, are you here?"

"I'm in here," I say, but just as he approaches my door, Sophia comes bouncing down the stairs.

"Like I said, you're just being paranoid," she yells. "There's nobody up there. I checked."

"Hold it, right there," the officer says, and I imagine him pointing his gun at my unsuspecting sister in the foyer.

I yell from my room with a croaky voice full of panic, afraid he might shoot her knowing the dispatcher likely told him I was alone in the house, "It's okay, that's my sister!"

The officer opens the door to my room, sees my condition, and gives me a look of sympathy as he lowers his gun from Sophia. "Are you saying she was upstairs the whole time making this noise you reported, and you didn't know she was home?"

"No, I heard something before she came back, when I was alone. I know I did!"

Sophia holds her hands up in front of her.

"I just checked both floors upstairs, and there's no one anywhere. She's on some heavy pain meds, and I think she may have imagined something, Officer. You're welcome to go check for yourself if you don't believe me."

The officer looks at us both and places his gun back in his holster. "I'll go look. You two stay in this room, and don't make a sound."

Ten excruciatingly long and silent minutes later, Sophia turns and gives me a frown full of pity as she stands in my doorway, speaking with the officer as he explains to her that he, too, found no one. My body has stopped sweating, but now I feel frozen solid in my saturated clothes even though I'm under my bedding and three other blankets.

After the officer gives Sophia his business card and leaves, she slumps her shoulders. "I'm going to get you something to help calm you down."

I wake at 2:00 a.m. in a cold sweat, and panic for a few seconds at my inability to move my wounded leg. The memory of my surgery usually comes back quickly after I wake, but I often relive the trauma as if it just happened.

Sometimes I cry until I fall back asleep, not knowing if my leg will ever be the same or whether I'll ever remember how the attack happened, and other times I just stare at the ceiling wondering how I got here.

Not having a clear plan for my life is slowly killing my soul and spirit, and I know it. But I don't know how to put myself back together again, not when I don't know how or why I fell apart in the first place.

When I reach toward my nightstand to grab my phone, I hear voices like before from upstairs. I consider calling out to Sophia, to see if it's her talking with someone else, but remember she conked out hours ago and never has anyone over. I chalk it up to the sound of the autumn breeze outside and ignore it, not wanting her to wake up and think I need another sedative to calm down.

My phone dings with an email notification, scaring a scream out of me before I can even think to cover my mouth. I take a slow, deep breath of relief after Sophia fails to come running downstairs to check on me and decide to open the email. But seeing the sender is a shock to my system. It's from Charlie.

Annette,

I miss you. So much. I wonder how you're doing all the time, and even though you gave me permission to, I don't want to move on. You're not a burden and you're not a chore. You're the one, and I want nothing more than to take care of you whether you're able to walk again or not.

Please take some time to reconsider my offer, and if you don't want to marry me anymore, I understand, but can we still be friends? I can't imagine not having you in my life at all, and I'm sorry about the Sophia stuff.

Congrats on the show. I ran into Monroe and she told me all about it. I'm writing a new thriller with Tim Watson, and I'm really excited about it. Tim Watson! I can hardly believe it! I just wish I could share it with you. Nothing is the same without you.

Love you always,

Charlie

Tears form behind my eyes as I picture Charlie's wounded face writing this email, and I forget about everything else that's been bothering me. I close my email, turn my phone face down on my nightstand, and roll over on my pillow. Only I hear something besides the sound of my sniffling, someone is talking again upstairs, and the voice sounds so familiar.

Whispers I can't make out now come from the air vent on my wall that leads all the way up to the attic, and if I didn't know any better, I'd say the voice I'm hearing sounds exactly like my mother's.

I plug my ears with my fingers as my shoulders quake, and I try my best to will the haunting whispers to leave me alone. I eventually cry myself to sleep with an achy chest, not knowing which is worse, my heart being shattered into a million pieces, or me losing what's left of my tortured mind.

"I really want to play up the house as a character. Maybe encourage the idea that it's haunted." Frank smiles as his eyes shift from me to Sophia.

Sophia stands up from the blue wingback chair in the library, then takes a sip of her sweet tea. "Oh, I like that idea!" She moves next to the fireplace mantel and pulls down the antique candelabra next to it. "Maybe we can pretend there's a secret passageway."

I can't help but giggle to myself knowing there actually is a hidden staircase no one knows about. Well, no one except Charlie and me. No one on set knew about it the whole time we filmed *The Night I Died*, and Charlie and I were stoked when we accidentally came across it in the library one day as we were building a fire.

I just happened to notice an emblem that was painted to blend in with the mantel a few weeks after I bought it. It looked like an old brass key wrapped in vines, and when I stroked it, it pushed inward. Then a door creaked open ever so slightly in the wall beside the fireplace, revealing a dark and dusty staircase that led to every other floor of the house.

"I never have thought the house was haunted. But it's funny you say all this now, because I'm beginning to wonder." I wheel myself to the doorway of the library where I peek into the hallway at the grand staircase. "I've heard some noises coming from our attic. Weird things."

Frank stands up and throws his hands in the air in a dramatic gesture of excitement. "Perfect! That's the kind of stuff I'm talking about. We need to give people the lingering suspense of *is it haunted, or isn't it?* Now, I think we all know it's probably not haunted, but there's no harm in allowing viewers to question it. Is there?"

Out of nowhere, Sophia starts humming a spooky tune as she dances around. "As long as we're pitching ideas ... we could also show off our other talents for viewers as well. I mean, they all know me from *Mindy and Missy Hart Do It Again*. I sang and danced through half of each show as the twins, maybe they want to see some of that again. After all, I'm not *just* an actress," she adds as I cringe.

"No, none of that singing and dancing nonsense, Sophia." Frank furrows his brows and shakes his head, nipping her idea in the bud before she has time to fully develop it in her own mind.

Sophia takes a seat in the wingback chair and crosses her legs with a grimace as Frank continues, "You sold me on you playing the part of the devoted, reformed sister, and that's what people want to see. Not you trying to act like twin little girls."

"I finally decided on the perfect title for the show after I got both of your contracts. I'm calling the documentary *Sisters of Crawford Manor*." Frank stands and uses air quotes around the title.

"So I definitely want to make the house one of the main characters. It'll really drum up interest from the cult following it has on its own. Plus, theorists can get a clear look at your inner circle of 'suspects' they think could've attacked you, Annette."

Sophia covers her mouth with one hand. "Oh, I love that, Frank. You're such a genius!"

She's not wrong. He is a cinematic and a marketing genius, but stroking his ego isn't the way to get what she wants from him. Frank is no nonsense, no fuss. And despite what she thinks, he sees through everything.

Frank looks to me for approval and reacts in no way to Sophia. "I think it's perfect, actually," I finally answer with a nod before he smiles and claps his hands together.

"Good, then we're ready to go. I'm going to get to work with the crew on setting up your cameras and connecting it to our streaming office." Frank makes his way out of the library and into the foyer.

"But don't forget, Sophia, any singing and dancing nonsense is going to get chopped on the cutting room floor. That's not what we're going for here. Just live your life like we said."

Sophia nods with a soft smile, but as soon as Frank lets himself out, she storms over to the library mantel and takes another huge swig of her sweet tea.

I start to wheel myself out of the library before she goes off on him, but she stops me with her words.

"Hey. The nurses aren't coming back anymore," she says in a low voice as I approach the doorway to leave.

I turn my chair around to face her. "What? None of them? But Doctor Lang won't be able to come for another week. Are you sure you can manage?"

"We'll figure it out." She slams her glass back down on the mantel so forcefully it sounds like it cracks. Then she saunters past me into the foyer, up the stairs, and inside her bedroom, where she slams the door so hard, I hear the picture of our parents fall off the hallway wall and break into a thousand pieces.

Chapter 4

"Help me, Annette," my mother whispers in my ear with a tone of distress. Her voice echoes in the room like it's coming down a tunnel far away, but I can feel her breath like she's right next to me until my eyes spring open. I'm awake, she's gone, and I find myself gasping for breath and dripping with sweat in bed.

Ever since the gas leak in my parents' house, I've had recurring dreams that my mom is whispering in my ear for my help, like I could have somehow saved them if I'd just thought to check the battery of their carbon monoxide detector the last time I was there. As if that were a normal thing to expect myself to do.

I reach for my phone to check the time, then guzzle some water from the glass on my nightstand. It's 7:00 a.m. on the dot, and Monroe will be here to pick me up at 9:00. There's no way I'm going back to sleep now, so I use my pillowcase to wipe the sweat from my forehead then rub my eyes with my knuckles.

After a month of practicing using my wheelchair, my arms are finally starting to get a little stronger, and I know if I want to be more independent, I must learn to manage more things on my own like Sophia said. So I muster all the strength I can and decide to wash my hair on my own. Even if it's the last thing I do.

"Annette! Wake up." I hear the faint voice of Monroe growing louder and louder in my head as warm water soothes my aching body. I open my eyes a little and make out a blurred version of her face as she lifts me back into my wheelchair. A dry towel is then draped over me, and she seemingly checks my head for injuries as her fingers dig through my hair.

"Are you okay? Did you pass out, fall, or fall asleep?" She has a tremor in her voice, but I'm just too groggy to answer her.

"I just slipped ..." I stammer as she grabs her phone and begins looking something up.

"No, no, no. I'm fine. I just slipped out of my shower seat after I was done washing my hair. I'm okay." I wrap the towel further around me and rub my throbbing shoulder.

"Wait, who are you calling?"

"Doctor Lang's office," she whispers with a shake in her voice as her phone rings on speakerphone.

"No, don't. I didn't even hit my head. I fell on my hip and my shoulder, and then I just laid there and fell asleep because I didn't get much rest last night. I guess the hot water just felt that good on my poor body," I beg as she reluctantly pushes end on her phone before anyone picks up.

Monroe raises her brows as she hands me another towel for my dripping hair. "You fell asleep on the shower floor?"

"I did, I swear," I explain, knowing if she calls Dr. Lang, I won't get to go out with her today on a much-needed excursion.

"If you tell him, I'll spend the entire day at the hospital or doctor's office wasting everyone's time checking for a concussion I couldn't possibly have."

Monroe hands me the clothes I laid out for myself last night as she thinks. "Well, if you're sure you didn't hit your head, then I guess it's okay."

"I'm sure," I answer with a smile. "And who's going to notice a few more bruises at this point anyway."

Monroe grabs her phone and shines the flashlight in my eyes to check my pupil dilation. "Well, I guess that's true, sadly. I was thinking we can stroll around Cove Park since it feels nice and sweater weather-y outside today, and then we can do lunch at Boho Bistro. Your fave."

I sigh with relief when she gives me a nod about my eyes and places her phone back down on the bathroom vanity.

"See, that sounds exactly like what I need. I mean, don't get me wrong, I love my house, but I *need* to get out."

Monroe snarls her nose as she picks up the hair dryer and plugs it in. "And away from that sister of yours."

◈

As soon as Monroe gets me out of the brand-new custom van—that she still claims she needed to disguise herself from the paparazzi and didn't have specially made just for me—we hear the distinct sound of cameras snapping nearby.

"Look! It's Monroe Jennings and Annette Taylor!" an excited fan screams from across the street as three paparazzi run toward us with their cameras up.

"Annette, you look great. Are you ever going to get back together with your ex-fiancé, Charlie Flynn? Are you hoping to walk again and revive your movie career, or is it true you have permanent nerve damage and a bad infection?" one paparazzo asks as he snaps his camera.

"Tell us about your new show with your sister," another man holding a video camera shouts.

Someone else screams a question to Monroe with no regard to my feelings as I blink back tears. "You're such a good friend. How does it feel to be at the peak of your career while your bestie is confined to a wheelchair?"

Monroe shoos them away with her free hand and curses under her breath as she pushes me faster toward the restaurant. Then, out of nowhere, a huge, muscular man with dark sunglasses runs down the street to our side, blocking the paparazzi behind us with his enormous body.

"Thanks, Big Joe," Monroe shouts to her favorite bodyguard over the voices of gathering fans as we approach the entrance to Boho Bistro. Normally, I'm excited to go inside because it means

I'm about to have a wonderful time, but today the restaurant simply feels like a safe haven from the wolves chasing us.

When we manage to get all the way inside the front door, the manager locks it behind us as Big Joe stands guard. Then we're placed inside an olive-green private booth next to a window viewing the garden in the back.

Lights are strung on the orange and red trees throughout the patio, and Moroccan rugs are laid out next to two fireplaces where several tables of happy people are living their best uninterrupted lives as we sit inside, confined for protection. The true price of fame.

"Can I get you anything?" the manager asks as another waiter quickly brings over a pot of coffee, two mugs, and two glasses of water.

I stare blankly at my menu without blinking because I can't process all that just happened. I knew my first real outing could be overwhelming, but I never imagined I'd feel this degraded.

Monroe takes one look at my face, pushes her menu away, and speaks for us both, "Just give us a few minutes, Mike. If you don't mind." She smiles, and he knowingly nods back.

"I am so, so sorry, Annette. I don't know why there would be paparazzi stationed here. They must've been tipped off. Did you tell anyone we were coming here?" She purses her lips.

I take a sip of water and think back to my texts from Sophia and Frank while we were at the park earlier and how I told them each separately where Monroe and I were eating for lunch.

"Just Sophia ... and Frank. But I don't think either of them would ..." I stop and think before I finish my sentence and decide I'd better not lie to Monroe.

"Of course, they would. Either one of them, or maybe both. Especially now, to get publicity out there for the show swirling around." She shakes her head in disgust. "And did I tell you Sophia already hit me up for a cameo earlier today when she let me in?"

"She didn't ..." I plant my face in my palm.

Monroe rolls her eyes and laughs. "Oh, but she did. Man, she's such a piece of work."

I take a deep breath as I digest what she said. "Not surprised, just embarrassed, I guess. I'm sorry she did that, but I really think she means well despite how she can come across."

"Don't be sorry. I'd expect nothing less of her. And besides, I told her I'd do it if you wanted me to—anything for my best friend. But I sure as hell won't be doing it for her benefit, that's for sure." She curls her lip.

I smile awkwardly, knowing why she feels the way she does and try to breeze past all the insults toward my sister. "I'd love for you to appear! But don't feel like you have to by any means."

"Anything for you. And I know this is awkward, but since you won't take me up on my offer to have you live with me ... I was thinking. I know you've spent a lot of money over the years on repairs for the house, digging your parents out of bankruptcy, rehab for your sister, and now on medical bills and taking care of your sister so she can take care of you. So if you need any help with expenses or anything…" She trails off, and I shake my head.

"No, seriously. I'm happy to help, and you wouldn't have to pay me back or anything. I just want you to be happy and taken care of."

I reach across the table, grab both of her hands, and squeeze them tightly as I look her in the eyes. "Thank you for saying that, but I'm okay. Well, for now at least. And this show is going to help me tremendously, I promise. But if money gets low, I'll reach out."

Monroe shuffles in her seat. "I hate that you're doing this show when you don't really want to."

I squeeze her hands again and maintain eye contact. "I hear what you're saying, trust me. And if things were reversed, I'd be offering you the same thing because I love you."

Monroe looks like she's close to tears. "But if it's just about the money…"

"It's not. Sophia's all the family I have left, and I know my parents would want us to reconcile and lean on each other. And this just feels right, even though it's really hard." I smile, knowing her good intentions and concerns are sincere and from the heart.

Monroe squeezes my hands one more time before we let go and she pours us each a cup of coffee. "Okay. I get that. But just know that as an only child, I think of you as the sister I never had, and I'd do anything for you."

I giggle as I make a stabbing motion with my knife. "I know you would."

She squints her eyes and lowers her voice before taking a big gulp of coffee. "So you can expect I'll be keeping an eye out on that *other* sister of yours."

After we've eaten, both our phones start buzzing over and over with alerts from multiple news sources. We eye each other and freeze with furrowed brows.

"Should we check?" Monroe asks as we reluctantly grab our phones and read the latest shocking headline.

"AWARD-WINNING ACTRESS DIANA RIVERS FOUND DEAD AFTER SINGLE-CAR ACCIDENT NEAR HER CALABASSAS HOME. POLICE SUSPECT FOUL PLAY."

"Oh my God!" I cover my mouth with my hand in disbelief and can't help but feel like I'm living in a real-life nightmare once it really sinks in.

Diana and I never got along because we basically competed for every role we ever had since we were young. We're both brunette, girl-next-door types, who are roughly the same age. She lost some parts to me, I lost some to her, but we were constantly pitted against each other in the media. So much so, we never actually became friendly like we probably should've.

"Okay, this is getting weird." Monroe's face goes white. "I'm seriously freaking out."

What if whoever attacked me is doing all this to these actresses like the rumors say. I mean that's just crazy talk, right? Surely Diana just had a freak accident, but God, you never know. Maybe someone ran her off the road on purpose or something.

My heart pounds in my chest and my head starts to spin. I feel dizzy, like I might faint as my mind continues to spiral ... *If someone wants me dead, why haven't they been successful yet?*

Monroe stops reading the articles online and dials someone on her phone. "That's it. I'm calling Big Joe in here. We're not going anywhere in public without him from now on."

And just like that, I can't help feeling strangely grateful that my house will soon be full of cameras watching our every move.

"When you push this button, the light turns from green to red. That means you've just turned this camera off. And when you push it again it turns green, meaning it's back on again," Frank says to me and Sophia while pointing to a camera on a corner desk in one of my guest bedrooms upstairs.

"I'm having them place all the cameras low so you won't have to worry about not being able to reach them, and then eventually we'll get you an app on your phone that can control them all."

But what he doesn't consider is the fact that each camera operates separately, so turning one off does nothing to all of the other ones in the same room. And based on what he's shown us so far, there are roughly four or five per room to catch multiple angles, depending on the size of the room. So, even if they *are* within my reach, it'll still be a lot of work for me to turn them all off until they get the app up and running.

"Do they automatically turn off once we're in bed?" I ask, hoping to God I won't have to go to all the trouble of turning them off every night because I don't want to be recorded sleeping.

Frank shakes his head. "They don't ever turn off unless you turn them off. Interesting things can happen in the middle of the night in an old, haunted house after all. I've already sent you both emails mapping out where every camera in the house will be placed, so you know."

I take a deep breath as I consider what I've gotten myself into, and Frank picks up on my hesitation. "Listen, I know this seems weird and feels like a lot, but it's a lot more private than being surrounded by a camera crew at all hours of the day and night."

A soft smile forms on my face, knowing he *is* right about that. "I know. I'm just starting to get nervous."

A male crew member who was setting up cameras downstairs runs in the bedroom and interrupts us with a nervous expression. "There's a lady on the intercom downstairs wanting us to open the gate. She told me where the button to open it is and she says she's Monroe Jennings. Do you want me to let her in?"

he asks Frank, and Frank turns to me with raised brows for an answer.

"Yes, please. That would be great. Thank you." I nod to the man.

"You're welcome, Ms. Taylor, and by the way, I'm a huge fan of yours. Well, and of Monroe's, too," he stammers, then gathers himself back together. "Hey, when you get a chance, could you come downstairs and let me test out some of the camera angles on you? I want to make sure I didn't place any of them too high for you to reach." The man then unravels some cords in his hand and looks nervous.

I smile. "Thanks so much for checking on that for me. That's so kind. I'll be right down." I begin to wheel out of the bedroom after him with a fresh sense of accomplishment for having gone upstairs to begin with. Just having this small change of scenery has helped soothe my soul for the day.

Sophia and Frank follow and help transport me from my wheelchair to the stairlift much easier than Sophia ever has by herself.

"See, Sophia, once Doctor Lang is here regularly, you'll have a much easier time getting me in and out of this thing."

Sophia grunts and grabs her back as I'm lowered down the stairs by the lift. "Oh, it's not so bad. Just doing my duty as a sister," she says in the kindest voice possible while eyeing Frank.

Monroe bursts through the front door as soon as we reach the bottom, but she wears an uneasy expression on her face that gives me pause.

"What's wrong?" I ask as Sophia and Frank transport me from the lift to the downstairs wheelchair.

Monroe shuts the front door behind her, but not all the way. "Did they tell you I brought someone with me?"

I look to Sophia who is walking alongside my chair toward Monroe with her hands on her hips. "No, why? Who's here?"

Monroe sighs and rubs the back of her neck with one hand.

"Gosh, I hope you aren't going to be mad. I didn't know it was going to be such a scene here today or I would've waited, but when I ran into him at the studio the other day we got to talking, and I couldn't say no when he asked if I could get him in to see you."

"You didn't dare bring *him* here, did you?" Sophia hisses, then looks to me to be equally offended as her eyes narrow.

The male crew member with the cords walks over again. "I'm ready for you, Ms. Taylor. Right this way. I'm Mark by the way." He points toward the sofas in the living area.

I gulp as all of the blood drains from my face. "Charlie?" I ask, and Monroe nods reluctantly as she bites her lip.

My throat tightens as I picture him seeing me—so pitiful in this chair. "I...I can't do this right now," I say, and wheel after the crew member whose name I didn't hear and head toward the other side of the great room.

But as soon as I arrive, I look back to Sophia and Monroe and notice they're now having heated words. A tall figure appears on the other side of the stained-glass front door and swings it open further.

"Ms. Taylor, can you reach this far?" the crewman asks as he points to a camera mounted on the wall. I force myself to look away from the chaos at my front door to pay attention to him.

"Oh, yes. That's fine." I interlock my trembling fingers together and squeeze to keep them still.

He heads over to the camera on the console table and turns it on. "Stay right there and don't move around too much. I'm just making sure it focuses correctly."

I glance toward the front door where Sophia and Charlie are now having minced words of their own and feel my heart rate start to soar. Charlie doesn't see me yet, but I spot the scruff on his face and his silky, shoulder-length brown hair and yearn for him to hold me in his arms again, despite everything I've done to push him away.

It's hard to make out their conversation with so many people roaming around the house talking, and drilling, but I try to listen as Sophia's wild arm gestures indicate elevating strife.

My one-hundred-year-old grandfather clock chimes twelve times by the front door, signifying it's lunchtime to the crew who all stop drilling when they hear it. All except the crewman still checking camera angles with me, that is. Everything in the house grows quiet except for the screaming match at the front door, and everyone turns to listen.

Sophia is in Charlie's face with a pointed finger as Monroe looks horrified beside him. Her eyes meet mine and widen with guilt for bringing Charlie here without checking first, as they should.

"My problem with you? My problem with you? Do you really have to ask what my problem with you is? It's your fault I got fired from *The Night I Died*," Sophia yells.

She's still convinced he had something to do with her firing because he was the head writer, and God knows she's not one who's quick to forgive and forget. Getting the boot from that movie cemented the end of her career, and she'll never get over it.

"I almost died that day! And then when I didn't, I woke up to find that everyone in Hollywood had written me off for good, and it made me wish I *were* dead." Sophia tears up as Charlie takes a step back with his hands out in front of him, blocking Sophia from coming any closer.

"No. I didn't have to do or say anything for the studio to fire you. You were belligerently drunk on set, and no one wanted to put up with you or another film plagued with your toxicity."

"I didn't drink. I was clean!" The large vein in Sophia's forehead protrudes.

Charlie takes another step away from Sophia, then drops his hands back down before he responds to her shouting with a calm tone, "You hadn't changed, and you didn't quit drinking. You picked your own noose out that day, and you have no one to blame but yourself."

Sophia raises a hand and sucks in a deep breath, seemingly ready to slap Charlie across the face before she slowly lowers it with a long exhale. Her cheeks grow pink as she clenches her fists by her side with a new purpose. She walks past Charlie with a strange look on her face and continues over to my antique grandfather clock where she gives it a gigantic shove.

The clock tips over in slow motion until it finally crashes to the floor, causing a shockwave of vibrations and deafening sounds of off-key notes throughout the house as everyone's jaw drops.

When it's finally quiet again, Sophia turns to Charlie with wild eyes as everyone looks on, afraid to say a word. "For the first time in my life, I was clean. You need to get out of this house, right now! Get out!" she cries at the top of her lungs.

It's then that I'm released from my temporary state of paralysis, and I start to bawl. And despite not wanting to draw attention my way, Charlie finally notices me in my wheelchair for the first time, looking like a blubbering idiot.

I wheel myself into the kitchen as fast as I can as tears freely flow from my eyes, and all I can do is thank God the cameras weren't rolling yet.

Chapter 5

I wake at 3:00 a.m. with an intense need to pee, so I manage to maneuver myself from my bed to my wheelchair, but as I approach my bathroom, I hear whispered voices coming from upstairs again. I open the door to my bedroom slowly and wheel myself toward the bottom of the grand staircase where I recognize one of the voices as Sophia's.

"Sophia?" I call in a worried tone, and the voices immediately go silent. "Is everything okay up there?" My voice shakes.

"I'm fine," she grunts. "I'll be down in a sec."

I wheel to the bathroom, pee, and get myself back into bed, still feeling like something's off upstairs. Then, the door to my bedroom opens slowly revealing Sophia's half-naked silhouette in the dark.

"Did you need something?"

"I just wanted to make sure you were okay. You've never had anyone overnight at my house before, and I ..."

"Yeah, I know. I have a guy here that I met a few nights ago," she says with a smirk.

I pause for a second and turn on my bedside lamp, not knowing how to redirect this conversation into something less uncomfortable. "It just sounded a little like …"

She interrupts me again, then waves her hands around as she turns to leave. "Yeah, I'm fine." But before she can turn away from the light, I catch a glimpse of red marks all over her wrists.

"God, Sophia. Your wrists. Are you sure everything's okay? I don't know that you should be letting strange men in the house, especially while there's an actress killer on the loose."

She sighs and rolls her eyes with irritation as she turns to face me. "I already told you, I'm fine. And he's not a stranger, exactly. Honestly, it's none of your business anyway. Just go back to sleep and don't worry about it. I'll see you in the morning."

Still unable to sleep, I check my email at 4:00 a.m. Frank sent more information regarding the show, and I'm anxious to read it. He set us up with functioning cameras all over the inside and outside of the house with an app where we can control them already. Filming officially starts in two days, but Frank says he and the other producers will be testing the cameras and capturing random footage on and off until then.

My eyes are burning, and it's only four thirty. I decide I feel safe enough to doze off despite the continued "sounds" of Sophia and her "friend" upstairs, because if he wanted to murder one of us tonight, he probably would've done it by now. I shut my eyes and start to drift off but hear strange, echoed voices in the attic through the slightly rusted vent in my room. I sit up straight in my bed and reach for my phone just as the muffled voices stop, and I wonder if I simply dreamt it before I lay back down and slip into a deep sleep.

When I ready myself the next morning, I call out for Sophia from the bottom of the stairs, only I'm left with the echo of my own voice bouncing off of the walls of the house with no answer.

I wheel myself to the window in my bedroom and peer outside to see if her car is missing from the driveway. Normally, she lets me know if she's going to go out, so I know when to expect her help with my meals and medication, but after the way she spoke to me and acted last night, I'm starting to get a pit of anxiety in my stomach that she's either in some kind of trouble or is upset with me for not minding my business.

Biting my nails, I notice a fresh glass of water, a pain pill, my antibiotic, and a note on my nightstand I missed before.

Here's the morning medicines you'll need, I'll brb. ——Sophia.

I go to grab my phone from under the covers where I left it last night but can't find it anywhere. I spend a ton of my already limited energy maneuvering my body around the room to look under pillows, the bed, in drawers, and on top of every piece of furniture in my bedroom and bathroom, but it's nowhere. And I'm worn out.

Would Sophia take my phone? There's no land line here anymore, and I have no other way to contact anyone without it. Maybe she wrote the note, mistook my phone for her own, and ended up with both by mistake. I give her the benefit of the doubt for an honest mistake, but still feel uneasy about being left in this house without a phone for God knows how long.

Even though I haven't eaten anything yet, I decide to go ahead and take the pain pill and antibiotic she left, afraid of the pain I'll be in without them. I remember Dr. Lang telling Sophia how important it was that I never miss a dose, because the pain that followed could be beyond what I could handle if I didn't keep it managed.

After eating two easy-access protein bars from the pantry and watching an old movie on AMC, my stomach churns so desperately for real food that I consider cooking some eggs while standing on one leg, even though I'm not supposed to. The wall clock in my room says it's 1:00 p.m. now, but according to my stomach, it's breakfast, lunch, *and* dinnertime, so I manage to get myself back into my wheelchair despite my weakened state and head toward the kitchen where I consider my options for lunch.

One simple bologna sandwich and a movie in the great room later, I head back to my bedroom where I swear I hear voices up in the attic through the vent again. I mute my bedroom TV and listen intently until I hear soft footsteps in the hallway upstairs. Tiptoeing.

My chest tightens when I realize they are headed toward the stairs leading down here. In a panic, I slide off of my bed and onto the floor, where I drag myself to my door to lock it just before a shadow approaches on the other side.

I hold my breath and scoot myself all the way into my bathroom to lock myself in and wait in terror for what they'll do next. The footsteps pause at my bedroom door right along with my heart, and I force myself to peek underneath the bathroom door where I see the outline of two brown work-boots outside my bedroom door.

When I finally allow myself to inhale again, my breaths burst in and out so fast I feel like I might die. I can't convince myself that the things I'm seeing and hearing are imagined or exaggerated in my mind this time. There's no way that the two feet standing outside my door simply don't exist, and as much as I wish I could, I can't dismiss what's happening in my home.

After an eternity of waiting for each other to make a move, I cry as silently as I can for my missing phone, and the footsteps slowly turn and begin to retreat to the stairs. I hear each agonizingly slow creak they make on both sets of steps as they ascend all the way up to the attic and disappear.

Too scared to emerge from the bathroom, I grab a few towels off of the vanity and make a place for myself to lie down on the hardwood floor as I do my best to curl up in the fetal position and not have a heart attack. The floor beneath me creaks and bows a bit as I nestle into a more comfortable position, and my still-racing heartbeat makes my entire chest and stomach burn.

I try my best to close my exhausted eyes, relax, and not have a full-fledged panic attack about it, though, because whoever or whatever was here is gone now. I'm as safe as I can be behind two locked doors, and there's nothing else I can do.

I'm going to be fine. I'm going to be fine. I'm going to be fine.

After what feels like another hour, I decide to see if any of the cameras happen to be on in my bedroom so I can ask the crew for help. I peek out of my bathroom only to be disappointed the lights on the cameras all are flashing red.

They probably did a camera check while I was in the bathroom knowing my luck. Still too afraid to leave my room, I slide myself over to the TV and turn it up while still being careful to keep it at a volume low enough that I can hear someone creeping up on me.

By four thirty I start to feel sick to my stomach. I start sweating and aching so badly from not eating enough that I dry heave on the floor. I guess my body finally had enough of pain medication, antibiotics, too little food, and crippling anxiety all mixed together. Nevertheless, I'm still too terrified to leave my room not knowing who or what may be waiting for me on the other side.

By five thirty I've officially given up hope for dinner. Sophia must've had something horrible happen to her, I decide, and she isn't going to be able to make it home at all tonight. I prop myself up against the foot of my bed and close my eyes as my stomach turns and gurgles, but I can't sleep even though I'm mentally and physically exhausted.

How long will I lie here helpless before someone finds me, until the cameras start filming our show in the morning? At least I know I won't die with no food for just one day. If I can make it 'til morning, things will get better. The cameras will bring help.

I picture Sophia being rushed to the ER after a car accident. "But my sister. My sister. She's home alone with no one to care for her. Send someone over right away to make sure she's okay." Then I laugh at how stupid it sounds.

She's probably out doing some last-minute shopping before filming starts tomorrow, or getting her hair done, not realizing she has my phone. Unless that guy last night really was abusive or is the serial killer? God, I hope she was telling the truth when she said she was fine and that he wasn't exactly a stranger.

At five forty-five I hear a car pull up the driveway. Then the front door bursts open with the sound of Sophia singing like she hasn't a care in the world as I lie on the floor next to my bed, weak and reeling with continued fear as she rustles bags around in the foyer. Shopping bags. *Guess I was right about it being something frivolous.*

"Annette, I have a surprise for you!" she yells once she's made several trips to and from her car to retrieve things.

She makes her way to my bedroom door like she has springs of excitement in her happy steps, but she pauses when she realizes it's locked. "Why's the door locked, Annette? Are you okay?"

She fumbles around, then produces a key from somewhere. And when she opens the door to my bedroom, she turns on the overhead lights. I squint and look up at her with disdain as she looks at me, smiling. "Wake up, sleepy head. I went shopping!" she says, entirely ignoring the fact that I must look like complete death here lying on floor.

I muster some words out with a frailty she doesn't seem to notice, then she plops down on the floor beside me with one of the shopping bags.

"Sophia, I'm sick. I've barely eaten anything today, and someone was in the house again. I swear. This time I'm sure I wasn't imagining it."

"I got you two new dresses you'll look divine in. Just divine!" Sophia glazes over my damage with a smile of denial, then cocks her head to the side with a look of disappointment when I continue to lie motionless in the floor. "Well, aren't you even going to look at them?"

"I need food, Sophia. And I've been so scared here today by myself," I say as tears stream down my face, knowing she won't understand.

She hops to her feet and heads out the door. "Okay, okay, okay. I get it. You're upset with me for leaving for too long. I'll go right now and make you your food, your highness," she says with a dismissive laugh, clearly not wanting to acknowledge the fact that I'm acting crazy again and being overdramatic.

When I sit up and peek inside the bag she brought in, I find two dresses in my size. With shaking hands, I hold up a blue

Michael Kors sheath dress and a pink, floral Free People dress. Both are beautiful and just my style, and I smile weakly as I struggle to hold them up to my pitiful little body. I guess she was trying to be thoughtful by shopping for me, and she doesn't want to hear what I have to say about what happened here because she feels like she'll have to tell Dr. Lang on me and up my meds.

She's never going to believe me unless she sees these things for herself, and I don't want to get myself committed or end up with a conservatorship for being delusional. Maybe she has the right idea by ignoring me, and I should just play along and keep quiet about everything that happened here today. It's not like the police are going to believe me either. But I can't ignore how convenient it is that these things are only happening when I'm here by myself.

Maybe it's just the meds making me loopy with too little food in my system, but I can't help wondering, *What if I really am losing it after the trauma I've been through? Do I really want that to be broadcast to the world on our show that starts filming here tomorrow?*

Chapter 6

Charlie kisses me. He holds me close to the warmth of his chest, and life is as it should be again. We stroll after dinner down a sidewalk downtown and come home to the house we both fell in love in, then build a fire in the library to roast marshmallows.

It's not just a dream, though; it's a glimpse of our old life together. One of those dreams where I know I'm dreaming but don't care because I'd rather live there forever than face reality.

Charlie and I creep up the narrow staircase hidden in the library wall and appear upstairs in the hall across from the guest bedrooms. A gigantic, old portrait of a woman who used to live here named Abigail Marshall hangs in front of the secret door.

But if you keep going up the spiral steps, it also comes out in the attic at another secret door within the paneling that's hidden behind an old dresser that belonged to my grandmother. Charlie and I are the only two people who know the passageway exists, and traveling up and down its secret world thrills us both as we carry an old oil lantern like Nancy Drew and a Hardy Boy.

We push cobwebs aside as we bypass the exit upstairs and keep ascending toward the attic. When we open the door, we find there's no dresser blocking the entrance anymore. Then Charlie opens the camouflaged door with a knowing grin, unable to contain the joy of surprising me. An enchanting oasis awaits with Christmas lights strung along all the walls of the attic, and my jaw drops when I notice a decadent dinner and a blanket surrounded by candles.

"Surprise!" Charlie opens his arms up to the room, presenting its new orderly fashion. All the boxes and furniture have been moved to one corner, the floors are cleaned up, and the space is now rustic but charming.

The dream is just as I remember it happening in real life, and I can almost smell the pumpkin candles burning on the attic floor as I relive everything that happened that day. We sit down and have salmon, broccoli, and baked potatoes while sipping champagne and talking. Raindrops start to tap on the roof, and Charlie opens the attic windows so we can hear their serene tune. They further exalt the ambiance of the house seeming haunted, but in an endearing way.

"I have something for you, by the way." Charlie pulls out a gift bag.

I furrow my brows, scared this is a present for some holiday or anniversary I forgot about.

"Just for being you." He hands me a big pink bag with a box inside.

I fiddle with the bag's tissue paper, struggle with the tape he wrapped around the box, and finally open it to find a piece of paper folded several times. I unfold it once, nothing, twice, nothing, three times, still nothing, and on the fourth time there's something for me to read. *Stand up.*

I look at Charlie with pursed lips as I continue to sit on the blanket. "Just do it," he says and smiles. And just as I stand, he gets up on one knee and pulls out a box from his back pocket. A small, black ring box.

I cup my mouth with my hands as I prepare to scream yes, but this time instead of getting happily engaged like we did in real life, a random handwritten letter appears on the blanket, catches fire, and causes the blanket to burst into flames with a single *whoosh*.

Charlie and I are both engulfed in violent flames that smother and scorch us, and we yell in agony as our bodies burn, but we can't escape because the attic walls are now closing in on us. The dream only ends when I wake myself up to the frenzy of my own silent screams.

My chest is tight as I sit straight up, and I can't catch my breath. Sweat pools underneath my body and soaks through the sheets as I smack the imaginary flames all over my body with my hands. When I finally realize I'm now awake, and not being burnt alive, I take a deep breath, close my eyes, and begin the process of calming myself down from my state of panic.

Images of the handwritten letter that started the fire won't leave my mind, and I feel like there's something about it that's important. Something my mind's trying to tell me. I close my eyes and try to picture the letter how it was in the dream but have no luck making out what it said. Maybe it has something to do with the night of my accident.

I still haven't been able to recall that night since it happened over a month ago. All I know for sure is that Charlie and I had broken up the day before, and Monroe had come by for a girls' night when she found me at the bottom of the stairs in a horrible state.

After a few more times of closing my eyes and trying to recall what the paper said, a flash of Dr. Lang and Sophia standing over me in my bedroom when I returned home from the hospital surges back into my mind. They're reading a similarly handwritten letter they pull out of an envelope with expressions of horror on their faces, but the memory ends there and fades to black.

Later that morning, my phone dings with a text from Grace. It's 6:00 a.m., only three hours until filming officially starts.

I'm so sorry, are you okay?

Her first text reads with a link to a *TMI* article, fresh off the press. It's always been the worst of the worst of online gossip magazines. They'll publish just about anything no matter who it hurts, especially if it's devastating or traumatic celebrity rumors.

I hope this won't make things worse, but I have to ask. Did Diana Rivers ever call or email you right before she died? She emailed me earlier that day asking for your phone number/email address, and I gave it to her, but she never said what it was for. I'm sure it's nothing, just a wild coincidence, but I was curious. Surely all this nonsense today from TMI *is lies, but I wanted to check and make sure you were okay. Let me know if you want to make a statement or anything.*

The link in the text is to an article titled "MONROE JENNINGS AND BFF ANNETTE TAYLOR'S EX-FIANCÉ, CHARLIE FLYNN, CAUGHT TOGETHER AT HER ENCINO HOME."

I pinch myself on the arm to make sure I'm not having another realistic nightmare, and it stings, but not as much as the article does. They go on to elaborate about their alleged secret hookup, and my heart races as I scroll through the details. Surely this is just a misunderstanding; *TMI* is wrong sometimes. Charlie would never, and Monroe would never. Or would they? Maybe things just happened one time they were alone, and they haven't had the heart to tell me they have feelings for each other.

Waves of nausea rise in my stomach, and I feel like I'm either going to faint or throw up. Even if it's completely innocent, the photo of them hugging inside her house all smiles without me looks terrible, and I can't handle being pitied in the press any more than I already have been.

Tears pool in my eyes and my cheeks are flushed with the embarrassment of once again being an easy target. I can't even imagine this being remotely true, but I guess some things you just never quite know for sure. TikTok fans are going to go nuts about this and accuse them of not only an affair, but my attempted murder as well. And of all days for this to come out, it had to spread like wildfire the day we begin filming our show.

In an attempt to think of anything besides the *TMI* article, I reread Grace's text about Diana and wonder what it could possibly mean. Why in the world would Diana Rivers ask for my contact information? We weren't even friends. I rack my brain to come up with a reason why she would try to reach out to me the day she died, but my broken mind once again fails me. I have no idea what's going on.

The lights on the cameras turn green right at nine, just after Sophia helps me get into my wheelchair. I can't help but feel like there's someone with us now that the cameras are rolling, and I'm thrown off with how extra sweet Sophia's being, until giving Monroe and Charlie a jab tempts her and suddenly, she isn't.

"I saw that *TMI* article about Monroe and Charlie this morning, and I have to say, I was shocked!" Sophia says directly in front of the kitchen camera at exactly 9:09 a.m. She could've said it in my bathroom when we were still off camera to spare me some humiliation, but she was clearly saving that little tidbit for the show.

I mean, I know this is what we signed up for and we're supposed to show our true lives, but starting the show like this right out of the gate makes me feel betrayed for the sake of hitting *them* where it hurts. Doesn't she realize this is a jab to me as well? Not to mention she would've been much more accusatory and ruthless toward them off camera. Calling them every name in the book behind their backs.

"It's laughable. Really. There's no truth to it," I say with a breezy tone, noting that if she wants to play with me on camera, I can play too. I *am* an actress after all.

"Oh, you're supposed to turn the vent on up there once the gas is going." I point above the range to the hood after she preheats the oven and pulls out a casserole dish. I guess she's going to act like she bakes something from scratch every morning on camera now, and I'm just supposed to go along with her facade as she airs my dirty laundry.

"I know that. I've been living here for weeks now." She smiles with a giggle as she grabs a mixing bowl.

"That's right, but this is the first time I've seen you attempt to bake anything since setting foot here." I give her a pointed look that lets her know I'm feeling triggered, and this isn't the way I want our show to go.

Sophia stays facing the range for a few seconds, seemingly composing herself and contemplating how she wants to respond. Finally, she turns to me with a grin and a hint of a clenched jaw.

"You're such a kidder, Annette. You know what, let's not talk about *TMI* right now anyway. Let's talk about something nice. How did you like those new dresses I got you?" She changes the subject.

But now I'm feeling paranoid about everyone in my life, including her. And I can't help but wonder if the sole reason she got those dresses for me was just so she could pat herself on the back for it later on film. Has she really changed like I think she has, or is she only interested in redeeming her image for her career?

"They were nice," I say with little enthusiasm as I continue to question everyone and everything. "Thanks."

Sophia cracks some eggs and mixes them in the bowl with cheese, sausage, and chopped green peppers. I wonder as I watch her if she thinks we must talk all the time now that the cameras are rolling, because neither of us is going to be able to keep this pace of conversation up without having a huge blowout over something we'd rather not mention to the entire world. And it's then that I realize just how difficult this process is going to be.

I decided against wearing one of the impractical dresses she bought me at Macy's and went for leggings and a sweatshirt instead. I'm not looking to impress people with an unrealistic or glamourous view of my life here at home right now. Like Frank said, the audience wants authenticity from us, and Sophia wearing a swing dress while baking a breakfast casserole from scratch ain't it.

When Sophia places the casserole in the oven, our childhood memories flash before me as the waves of heat escape the oven ...

❖

Mom is in the kitchen cleaning up after breakfast on a Saturday, and Dad's helping Sophia pack her bags for another day of filming her hit show *Mindy and Missy Hart Do It Again*. I'm watching him gush all over her like the child-star she is even though she just threw a gigantic tantrum about eating her breakfast that ended with her throwing a pancake at Mom.

"I don't like this new attitude, Sophia. Just because we allow you to work doesn't mean you can treat everyone like you're better than them." Mom scowls toward Sophia and Dad.

Dad looks at Mom with big eyes that seem to say, *"Don't tick her off right before we leave."* But often, no matter what time it is, he allows Sophia to get away with whatever she wants. After all, he knows she makes more money than he does. *And looking back now, I realize the newfound pressure on Sophia to continue to succeed must've felt very heavy for her at times, despite her bratty behavior.*

"Remember, positive attitude with a bright smile! Let's grab McDonald's on the way to work instead," he says to Sophia before they walk out the front door, and he neglects to acknowledge me at all.

"We'll stop and get you your favorite donut when we go to the store, Annette. Okay?" Mom walks over to me at the kitchen table where I sulk over my clean plate.

"How about we go look at those puppies down at the pet store, too, while they're gone?" She pinches my chin and gives me a grin seemingly trying to cheer me up.

I start to smile, then frown. "But won't Daddy and Sophia be upset they didn't get to go?"

"Eh. They'll get over it when there's a cuddly new puppy in the house to love on," she says as she walks over to a drawer to get her cleaning cloth. "They have their own thing going on anyway. Go get ready, and we'll leave in an hour or so."

"You mean we're actually going to get one?" I run over to her and jump up and down as she scrubs the stovetop.

"If there's a puppy we fall in love with." She turns to eye me with a wink.

"I'll go get ready right now!" I dash upstairs faster than I ever have in my life, not knowing that just a week later I'd be absolutely devastated when I walked in my room expecting to find my brand-new, adorable puppy playing with his toys, only to discover him dead instead.

Sophia calls my name loudly, like she's already said it more than a few times, and I'm pulled from the painful, distant memory.

"Annette?"

I jump. "Yeah."

"What are you doing? I asked if you were going to answer your phone. It's been over there lighting up and vibrating like crazy." Sophia looks concerned as she stares at me with wide eyes.

"Oh. Yeah. Sorry. I was in a deep thought for a minute." I grab my phone and see I've missed four calls from Monroe and two from Charlie. Then I close my eyes, feeling unmotivated to deal with this *TMI* problem on camera, while also knowing it's a part of what I've signed myself up for.

Our contract states we are to converse via speakerphone with parties who signed off on being guests on the show, so I'm already dreading this conversation. Sophia walks behind me to view the missed calls for herself, and I can't believe a story this big has already hit during filming. It's only day one, for Pete's sake.

Sophia winces and starts to speak slowly like she has bad news, "Oh, by the way. I talked to Frank this morning, and he said he asked Charlie to sign on as a guest yesterday since you two have such a history, and the paperwork came through almost immediately. So, Charlie's fair game for filming if you decide to call him back."

I'm torn between ripping the band-aid off now or waiting, but I know the longer I stall the more I'm going to make myself miserable. So I wheel myself into the library, shut the door, and take a deep breath.

Monroe answers my call on the second ring. "Oh, thank God! I was so afraid you wouldn't call me back," she says sounding out of breath.

"You're on speakerphone and we're being filmed, just so you know," I remind her as a brand-new knot of worry forms inside my stomach.

She breathes a little less heavily this time. "Yeah, yeah. I remember."

I furrow my brows. "What are you doing?"

"Went out for a run to clear my head. This *TMI* shit is really getting to me. Are you okay? You don't actually believe any of this, do you?" she asks, not sounding overly concerned.

"No…" I start with hesitation, not wanting my voice to sound shaken up, "but I'd like to know what *was* happening in those photos." I say, surprised I'm able to finish with an even tone.

Monroe takes a deep breath. "You sound upset. Listen, I'm so sorry for how it looks. But I swear, he just came over for about an hour to discuss you. He wanted me to try and arrange a different way for you two to get together after the other day went so badly. We hugged before he left. Right by the window out front, unfortunately, and someone got the shot, that's it! No lies, no alcohol, no secrets, no hookups. Nothing shady."

I take a second to digest what she's said and ultimately decide I believe she's telling the truth. "Okay. I mean, all of that makes sense."

"I promise, I'd never hurt you like that. Never in a million years. Damn *TMI* for making you question that. They love to fill the narrative with whatever will get them the most attention," she fumes, with an irritation I share.

"Believe me, I know," I huff, remembering the many times they got unflattering shots of me at the beach and insinuated I was pregnant.

"Charlie's been trying to get ahold of you, too. He's so messed up over this. The media's really coming after us both hard, and he's not doing well. Do you think you might call him?"

I take a moment to pause and think. *Should I call him? Should I deny this story publicly in some way and protect the two of them?* Then I picture him tossing and turning in bed at night not being able to sleep until he knows I believe him.

"Yeah, I'll give him a call. Make sure he's okay."

Then the sound of glass breaking outside the library door startles me, and I jump. "I've got to go. I'll call you later." I start to hang up and wheel toward the door.

"Love you," she quickly says with a warm tone.

"Love you, too," I reply, recognizing that I still sound a bit unsure.

When I arrive at the library door, I fling it open into the foyer where Sophia's picking up pieces of my blue-and-white candle.

"I was dusting and it fell," Sophia stammers, and I think it's safe to assume she was "dusting" the table to eavesdrop.

"That's weird. I don't think I've ever seen you dusting here before." I grin as I wheel past her into the foyer and out the front door where I bring Charlie's contact information up on my phone and take a deep breath.

Chapter 7

The air outside is cool and refreshing, and a gust of wind blows crimson leaves all over the twenty-two acres of land surrounded by iron gates. I look over to the line of black rocking chairs beside me and remember all the times I sat here with Charlie by my side, and selfishly, I still want him here to hold my hand and help me navigate this never-ending nightmare despite the things we couldn't agree on.

Selflessly, I want him to move on and live the life we planned with someone else, because this isn't what he signed up for. Hiking, tennis, water skiing, rock climbing—all the active things he loves—will be impossible for me, on top of all the Sophia stuff.

Why should he have to give up everything that makes him happy and put up with Sophia because of me? The answer is simple ... He shouldn't. Plus, I figure if I give him enough time and space, he'll realize that on his own.

However, I'd be lying if I said I don't have hope I can overcome what I've been dealt and eventually come to an agreement with Charlie about having Sophia in my life. Maybe a miracle surgery or drug will come out soon that can fix my damaged body and things can go back to normal or, if given enough time, Sophia and Charlie can finally accept each other. But for now, I owe him distance.

I pull out my phone and tap on his name with a shaky finger, but when I click call, I don't immediately put the phone up to my ear to hear it ring. Instead, I stare at the letters that spell out his name. A name I haven't allowed myself to really say, think, or even look at in what feels like so long.

"Annette?" I hear his voice say from a faraway place I can't quite reach, and for a second, I wonder if this was a huge mistake and I should just hit end. It seems like he answered on the first ring, and I find myself somehow feeling caught off guard even though I'm the one who made the phone call. I refrain from saying something under my breath as I bring the phone to my mouth and ear, then take a deep breath, preparing myself to hear his voice at full volume. I can do this. I can just be his friend.

"Yeah, Charlie. It's me," I finally answer as he sighs with relief.

"I'm so glad you called me. I swear nothing's going on with Monroe and me. I wanted to talk to her about trying to see you again. I promise. That's it!" Charlie spouts without taking a breath, like he won't ever get a chance to tell me again.

I interrupt before he spills every detail of their meeting like he does when he's worried. "Charlie, I already talked to Monroe, and she explained it all to me. So don't worry, I believe you. It's just *TMI* being *TMI* again."

"Oh, thank God! I don't know what I'd do if you didn't believe us. I don't want ..." Charlie starts to overshare again, but I stop him.

"Besides, if you want to move on with someone, you don't owe me any kind of explanation anyway. I've already told you to live your life. I'm the one who ended everything." I gulp with a grimace, the taste of my lies not going down easily.

Charlie pauses before responding, and my heart stops. I wonder if he's afraid to tell me he's already moved on, just not with Monroe. "Well, I don't see any reason we can't be friends after all we've been through together," he finally says, and I take in a breath. "I mean, what's the harm in trying?"

I chew on my fingernails, not knowing where to go from here because he does have a point. Then, I decide just to be honest. "I'm not sure I know how to be just friends with you. I mean, how would we even start?"

"Well, people get divorced all the time, and if they have kids, they still have to deal with each other. They eventually become friends a lot of the time after they've had time to grieve and move on. Er ... No ... Scratch that. Don't think of it that way because we aren't stuck with each other ... That's not what I meant."

Charlie starts to ramble, and I can't help but smile, missing his nervous bantering back and forth with himself.

"Just treat me like I'm Monroe. Let me help you out with all the things she helps you out with," he says with enthusiasm, as if this could work, and work well.

Although I picture the catastrophic ending this is sure to cause when it doesn't, in fact, work well, it doesn't stop me from shrugging my shoulders and agreeing that it's worth the risk. Just hearing his voice today has already changed my mind, despite my better judgment.

"Well, I guess we could try." I bite my lip, knowing this is probably a huge mistake.

"Okay. Well, to start ...Why don't you tell me how you've been. How you've *really* been?"

I take a deep breath, trying to decide how honest I feel comfortable being. But then again, I don't know how much he's already been able to pry out of Monroe.

"I've been okay, I guess," I lie, still wanting to save face on some level.

"I mean, being with Sophia has its challenges for sure, and coming to terms with all that's happened to me has been difficult. But ... I'm still here at least."

Charlie gives me a sympathetic sigh, "Yeah. I know it's been beyond tough on you. You've been through some real trauma, and trust me, I know you need your space as far as a romantic relationship goes. But I mean it when I say I'm here for you. However you'll have me."

"I appreciate that." I grin and my cheeks grow warm at the thought of his continued longing to be more than friends with me despite my limitations.

"How have *you* been? I know you have a lot going on."

"Honestly, horrible. It broke my heart when you called off the engagement. Then this terrible thing happened to you, and you cut me out of your life," he says with a wounded bluntness you can't fault him for.

"I know," I whisper, eyeing my mangled leg in shame even though he can't see me. I didn't do any of this to hurt him, but I know I have.

"I'm sorry. It's just with my parents gone I fell into a crisis, pushed you away, and felt this innate need to bring Sophia back into my life. Then, when I brought it up to you, we broke up, and all this craziness happened, and I finally had a reason to reach out to her."

"I'm not sharing to make you feel bad. I'm telling you so you understand I'm in love with you no matter what's happened to you or who you let into your life. I'll do as you ask and just be your friend, but you need to know how I really feel." His voice quivers with pain.

I sit in silence as I shove down the lump in my own throat. "Let's just see how we do as friends for now."

"Okay. I can do that," Charlie says with a small smile of hope I can hear through the phone.

Sophia's high heels clack from my bedroom to the kitchen after an exhausting morning of chatting a million miles per hour. I pull the covers over my face, turn the cameras off, and close my eyes for a much-needed nap. Sophia's clearly had one too many cups of coffee today, and I'm already worn out.

A fog surrounds me as I run through the damp grass searching for something in the dead of night. I'm desperate for it, and it pains me not only emotionally, but physically as well. When I reach our house, I run to my bedroom where I think I'll find it, but crawl in my bed and bury myself under the covers instead.

The sound of the walls creaking and splitting around me are deafening, but I don't dare peek from the covers because I know if I do, the monster will consume me. I plug my ears with my fingers as a familiar tune plays, one I haven't heard since I was seven years old. The song Sophia used to sing to me when I had a bad dream in the middle of the night. *Hush, Dear Sister.*

She used to cuddle up next to me and sing me back to sleep as she covered us both up with my comforter. *Hush, Dear Sister, just close your eyes ... sissy's right here, so don't you cry.*

The tune soothes me just like it used to, and I forget the walls of my cherished home are closing in on me and shut my eyes. But they crash into me anyway just the same.

My upper body jerks when I wake, and I'm covered in sweat again. I reach for the water at the side of my bed, but a thought suddenly hits me. It's been well over a month since my accident—plenty of time to mentally adjust, at least subconsciously—but my injuries have failed to follow me into my dreams. In fact, it seems I'm always physically running from something with perfectly healthy legs. Wonder what that means?

Sophia's wheeling me down the hall toward the theater room with a blindfold around my eyes as if I can't tell exactly where she's taking me. I've lived here for fifteen years and know every inch of this house by heart no matter how many circles she spins me in. Every creak in the floor, hole in the wall, loose nail, crooked painting, and squeaky door. There's no fooling me in my own home.

It's all for show anyway, so I play along just to make her happy. The cameras are rolling, it's the third day of filming, and Sophia's got something up her sleeve. She's grown moodier since the show began, and I'm beginning to grow concerned she's going to completely fall off the wagon if she can't regulate her system.

She's overly peppy in the morning and afternoon, groggy after dinner, and downright crabby and exhausted at night by the time she goes to bed. I often hear pacing in her room late at night, too, like something's royally messed up her sleeping patterns.

Maybe she has a personality disorder she's unaware of, I don't know. But for now, I'm trying to focus on the extra care and attention she gives me while the cameras are rolling. I've learned in the past that trying to have honest conversations with Sophia about her toxic habits and behavior never ends well, and I don't want to push her away now that we're finally getting close again. Besides, I don't know everything. Maybe this is normal for her.

"Okay, you can take the blindfold off now," she says with a high-pitched voice full of excitement.

"Oh, wow!" I say as I take in my newly decorated theater room. Posters of our movies and TV shows now line the walls like it's a real theater, and Sophia looks like she might burst with excitement.

"What do you think?"

I smile back and can't help but notice that she gave herself three more posters than she gave me. "I love it!"

"Good, because I have another surprise. I found these old episodes of *Mindy and Missy Hart*, and I thought we'd watch a few while we drink our morning coffee."

She wheels me to the front of the room and parks me in place as I plaster on a fake smile knowing I don't exactly have a choice but to grin and bear it.

"Aww. How fun!" I act my ass off.

Sophia runs to the back of the room to ready the big screen, and I close my eyes and try my best to mentally prepare myself for what's coming. The *Mindy and Missy Hart* show was like a combination of the music from *Annie* mixed with Punky Brewster's sass. Adorable to some, and nauseatingly annoying to others. Mindy and her twin sister Missy were polarizing characters, kind of like Caillou was, and I can only hope Sophia won't resort to ... Too late.

"And I know, that as I grow, I will turn into my own tomorrow ..." Sophia sings and dances along to the theme song, and somewhere in L.A. Frank's head is going to implode when he sees this. I nod and smile as she continues to perform, knowing it'll be worth my while to mind my p's and q's on this one.

Sophia's feeling nostalgic after a tiring day of reminiscing about everything *Mindy and Missy Hart*. She's held my hand, rubbed my shoulders, and kissed me on the head several times today, and I don't know what to make of it. Maybe she's excited Dr. Lang starts coming to the house tomorrow to care for me, or maybe she truly had fun. But after I help her clean up the kitchen and wheel myself toward my bedroom, I notice her giving me a funny look.

"Annette, I was thinking ... I'm tired and don't really want to go out tonight. What if I spent the night in your room and we have a slumber party like when we were little."

Why is she asking me this now? Frank texted earlier that they had updates to run on the camera software, so they'll all be turned off for the night.

"Sure, that might be fun. Hey, thanks again for putting all those old posters up. That was really thoughtful." I smile, and mean it, because it feels like the first day we've really been a team, even if it was coaxed by the cameras and Sophia's need to talk about herself all day.

"I'll grab some snacks. And you're welcome for the posters. I enjoyed doing it," Sophia says as she heads toward the kitchen.

"Want some wine or just seltzer water?" Sophia yells from the kitchen. "Don't worry, no wine for me."

"Both?" I laugh as I wash my makeup off in the bathroom, stopping dead in my tracks when I think I see my mom's face in the mirror behind me.

I scream, and my body starts to shake as I look all around me for a ghost that isn't there. The floorboards creak upstairs over my head, and I try to catch my breath and count to ten before Sophia comes running in to see what made me yell.

It must have been soap in my eyes or something that made me think I saw Mom; probably because I keep having those nightmares about her and Dad. I blink a few more times and look in the mirror again to see that all is as it should be and decide it must have been in my head.

Sophia arrives a few seconds later with food and drinks in tow. "Did you just scream?"

I splash cold water on my face from the sink again and try to steady my breathing. "Yeah, the water was too cold at first."

She lays everything down on my nightstand, then plops down on my bed and opens a can of water for herself.

"Well, I grabbed cabernet for you, popcorn, and some seltzers."

"You have an oversized T-shirt I can borrow so I don't have to go back upstairs?" she asks as I wheel over to my dresser to grab something to sleep in.

"Yeah, sure. Here you go." I toss her a vintage Britney T-shirt.

She strips her clothes off unapologetically, revealing her porcelain white skin and fat-free body. I carefully remove my own clothes and frown at my skinny, untoned body as she sings a Britney lyric.

It's only been a few weeks, but I swear I can see my leg muscles shrinking down to nothing by the minute. Amazing how quickly something can deteriorate that took years of hard work to build up.

"Did you see the latest about Diana?" Sophia asks as she helps me get settled into bed then shuts the door.

"No, what?" I perk up, feeling scared of what she might say while also wishing I knew why Diana tried to get ahold of me. Even though I've searched and searched, I never found any emails, missed calls, or voicemails from her. She must have died before she had a chance to reach out, so I guess I'll never know.

"Apparently, someone cut the brakes to her car, and *that's* why she had the wreck. Isn't that insane?" she scoots closer with a blanket.

My shoulders tense up and blood slowly drains from my face because I know in my gut these deaths aren't unrelated coincidences. Nobody can deny this appears to be the start of a clear pattern, and it sure seems like those wild conspiracy theorists on TikTok, who other people were making fun of, were on the right track. Someone *is* coming after actresses, and they're doing it in all sorts of unpredictable ways.

While I'm scared for myself, I'm also scared for Monroe and Sophia. Who's to say we won't be next. And who's to say the cameras will always keep us safe.

It's three in the morning when I wake with a headache and notice drool pooled on my silk pillowcase. I feel like I had three glasses of cabernet instead of one, and I can hardly form a thought I'm so groggy. I grab two ibuprofen from my night stand, not wanting to face the wrath of an even worse headache later, but as soon as I swallow the pills, I hear a thud upstairs.

The ceiling shakes on the right-hand side of the room, and Sophia wakes up next to me. She stirs and looks over at me with furrowed brows, surprised I'm awake.

"Did you hear that upstairs?" I ask, and she shakes her head no, then closes her eyes again.

The sound of what must be a heavy piece of furniture being dragged across the floor upstairs or maybe even in the attic sends chills up and down my body, and when I turn my lamp on, I notice my bedroom door is now wide open. I could've sworn Sophia shut it though.

"What the hell was that?" I whisper in Sophia's ear as she opens her eyes with an annoyed expression.

"You!"

"No, there's something being dragged somewhere upstairs. Something heavy. Listen!" My eyes dart back and forth as I study the ceiling for movements.

"I don't hear anything." She reopens her eyes and stares at the ceiling for a few seconds. If she's lying, she's doing a really good job. Either she truly doesn't hear anything, or she's still half asleep and doesn't care. Either way, I'm now questioning my own sanity even more than I already was.

My eyes burn and grow heavy, and I feel disoriented in a way I never have before. Time seems to move at a slower pace, and my mind can't focus. Maybe I'm just tired and overstressed about the things I think I'm hearing in this house, or perhaps there *is* something supernatural going on here. Maybe my accident, Sophia moving in, and all the cameras being set up here stirred up a spirit that's been lying dormant here for years. But why am I the only one who can sense it?

I wake again at four and shiver. Sophia's still sound asleep, the cameras are still off, and I'm surprised I can't see my breath in this frigid air. It must be fifty degrees, and I notice my bedroom door is now shut. Maybe the heat went out from a power outage and Sophia shut the door when I was asleep.

Only, when I look at her, she's in the exact same position she was in when we last talked, and I don't get the impression she's been up at all. Against my better judgment, I pull another blanket over my face from the foot of the bed and try to go back to sleep, however I can't shake the distinct feeling that we're both being watched by someone ... or something.

Chapter 8

My head is splitting when I wake up at six. Sophia's still dead to the world, so I grab the pain medicine on my bedside table and take it early. After I style my hair and throw on some makeup, a faint knock at the front door startles me. Dr. Lang isn't supposed to be here until eight, but it must be him. Maybe Sophia gave him the gate code already.

I wheel myself down the hall, where I try to make out the silhouette behind the stained-glass door, but I still can't tell who it is. Just as I turn back around to go wake Sophia up, the doorknob turns and the front door cracks open, and I hear my mother's voice.

"Hello? Annette, Sophia? The door was unlocked, so I just let myself in. I hope that's okay."

I cover my ears with my hands and shut my eyes, convinced my mind must've been playing tricks on me. *That voice wasn't real.*

And when I open my eyes again, I don't see my mom. Instead, I see Dr. Lang walk into the foyer with his medical bags.

I blink again and my pulse stops racing once I realize it really is Dr. Lang in front of me, and then I try my best to act normal. "Hi, Doctor Lang, come on in. Sophia's still sound asleep, but I could use a hand with breakfast if you're up for it."

Dr. Lang hangs his hat on top of the coat rack beside the door, passes the grand staircase, and meets me in the kitchen to help. "I've been meaning to tell you. You should look into the new lift systems they have now. The ones where you don't have to switch from your wheelchair to the lift chair. You can just use your wheelchair in and out."

"I've seen them, but they're so expensive and I'd hate to damage these old stairs. It'd be worth it if I end up being in this thing permanently, but I feel like getting one would make it official that that's going to be the case," I say, knowing how much easier it *would* make getting around this house.

"Sophia got this system from someone super cheap because right after they bought it the person they got it for died."

Dr. Lang nods, looks toward the front door, and changes the subject. "I do hope everything is okay. I assume you two don't routinely go to sleep with the front door unlocked."

"God, no. Or at least I don't think we do. I guess Sophia was in a rush to get to bed last night and forgot. Usually it's always locked," I assure him, but I also can't help wondering if that's why I've been hearing noises. Has Sophia been acting this careless often?

Someone still would've had to get past the gate to enter the house, but there are ways to do that if you really want to. But for the love of Pete, there's an actress murderer out there. You'd think she'd be more careful since there are two in *this* house.

I look around the kitchen to make sure all the cameras are flashing green after last night's software update. "Just so you know, Frank said he got all your paperwork for filming, and you're good to go. All the cameras are up and running already, so just know that you're being recorded."

Dr. Lang looks around with a concerned expression, probably wondering how many cameras there are in the house. Maybe he's having second thoughts about being thrown in our fishbowl with us.

"Want some tea?" I grab two mugs on the counter and fill them with water from the refrigerator door. The stevia and tea bags are also down low in a cabinet where I can reach them along with a few other snacks and basics. Sophia must've been feeling generous when she rearranged things for me, or maybe she was just ready for me to make my own damn tea already.

"Of course. Tea *is* the drink of my people you know." He laughs, and even though I'm not specifically attracted to Dr. Lang, I do agree with the theory that British accents make any man sexier.

"I'm sorry I came a bit early. I have an eleven o'clock patient at the office today. But now that I'm here, it looks like you're adjusting quite well." He has a seat at the kitchen table and crosses his legs as he takes a good look at me.

I wonder if the way I make my tea in the microwave like an American peasant is making him cringe. I bet he's dying to pull out a kettle, a saucer full of sugar cubes, and a fancy serving tray, but he holds his tongue, nonetheless.

"Yeah, it hasn't been easy. But hopefully with you here I can get better even faster." I smile as his mug of water heats up.

"I still have hope I can walk again. I mean, I have to have hope, or what's the point?" I shrug, surprised at how comfortable I am speaking so honestly with him.

"I realized yesterday in my dreams I can walk. Do you think that's strange or means something?"

He eyes me with a puzzled expression. "Well, I think there's always reason to hope, and it could be a good omen, but I will say, I've heard it can take your subconscious mind a while to adjust to life changes."

"Oh, really?" I say, still waiting for the humming microwave.

Dr. Lang crosses one leg over the other and shakes one foot. "Yes. For example, if you move into a new house, you may dream about your old house for as many as ten to fifteen years before the new one starts showing up. And even then, you might get the architecture wrong for a while."

I scrunch my brows and try not to feel discouraged. "But everyone's mind and body are different."

Dr. Lang uncrosses his legs and leans forward with a smile. "Of course, you're a hundred percent right on that, and given the right treatment or surgery, anything is possible. That's one thing I've learned from practicing medicine for twenty-something years. You never know what's going to come out in terms of medicine, and you should never underestimate what the human body can do when a patient has a strong will."

The microwave dings, so I take his mug out, place it on the table in front of him, and put mine in. Sounds of movement upstairs let me know Sophia has finally woken up and she's gone to her room to get ready.

"Well, I'm willing to put the work in. Whatever it takes. That's what's different about me now. A month ago, I wanted to give up and disappear. Now, I want my life back, even if things look ... different."

Dr. Lang fixes his tea and places his hand on mine, and it feels strangely natural. "Ah, then I think that's a recipe for success. Don't you? Hope for the best but be okay with what you're dealt."

The loud buzz from the gate's intercom makes me jerk my hand from his. "Sorry, someone must be at the gate," I say, then wheel over to the intercom, confused about who else could be here.

"Who is it?" I ask, still feeling flustered about our hands touching.

"Hey, I'm glad you're up. It's me and Charlie. He knows the gate code, of course, but I just wanted to give you a heads-up that we're here," Monroe says, and I find myself sweating. A heads-up would be letting me know they're coming *before* they showed up, not when they're already here.

A plethora of thoughts immediately race through my mind as I look to Dr. Lang and wince. Why on Earth are they here, and why are they *always* together? And, damnit, I left my phone in my room again. She probably *has* tried to call and text me about their drop-in.

"Okay, umm ... Well, I guess I ... I'll see you all in a minute, then," I say with little enthusiasm to Monroe, then turn to Dr. Lang.

"I'm sorry, I didn't know they were coming."

"Not to worry. I only planned to get acquainted with the house and set up a few things with you. If I can still leave here by ten thirty, I'll be fine."

Sophia's continued footsteps make the floors creak upstairs, and she calls out to me, "Annette, are you down there with Doctor Lang?"

"Yes, and Charlie and Monroe just pulled up," I yell back, and I can almost hear the curse words Sophia says in her head. No doubt she's going to be pissed.

"Alright. I'll be down in a few minutes," she answers in an annoyed tone, and I wonder what series of four-letter words she would've used if the cameras weren't rolling.

"So, what all did you want to set up with me today, Doctor Lang?" I ask, hoping I won't have to do anything too embarrassing on camera.

He places a hand on top of mine once again. "Well, first of all, since we're old friends, I'd like for you to start calling me Spencer. We're going to be spending a lot of time together from here on out, after all. Unless that makes you uncomfortable, of course."

"You know what, I think I can do that. Even though it might be a little weird at first." I stick out my hand to shake on it, but he ends up closing both of his hands over mine and holding it.

Monroe shuts the front door, and I see Charlie staring our way from the foyer.

"Hey, the door was unlocked," Monroe calls as she hangs her coat and bag on the rack, and I pull my hand from Spencer's.

"I didn't realize you had company." Charlie clears his throat in the uncomfortable way he does when he feels nervous.

"Yeah. Me either." Sophia makes her way down the stairs. "It seems I'm late to the party." She laughs with a perturbed expression as she reaches the foyer and makes her way toward Spencer and me in the kitchen.

How she's managed to go from dead to the world to looking fabulous in ten minutes, I'll never quite know. Her hair is in a chic bun, her makeup is minimal but on point, and her slim figure looks fantastic in her boho-chic, bell-sleeved dress.

"Well, you cleaned up nice today, Annette. Look at you!" She winks, breezing past Charlie and Monroe as if they don't exist, and hands me my phone. I look down at my black leggings, sneakers, and blue sweater, and shrug with confusion as I take my phone and say thanks.

"No, silly. Your hair and makeup! They look great!" She draws a pretend circle in the air around my head.

"Oh, thanks," I say, but she's already turned her attention toward Dr. Lang.

She bends to air kiss him on each cheek. "It's so great to see you, Spencer."

"I'm so glad you're taking such great care of things down here, Annette." She affectionately plays with my hair behind me like I'm a child.

"Charlie, Monroe ... tea ... coffee?" she asks loudly, because Charlie's still standing at the door with his coat on.

"We can go if you're busy. Maybe another time would be better ..." He starts to walk back out the front door, only his ride is now making her way into the kitchen with confidence.

"Oh, you must be the infamous Doctor Lang. Hi, I'm Monroe Jennings." She zeros in on Spencer with an outstretched hand.

"I've heard such wonderful things about you from Annette, and I'm so glad you'll be taking extra care of our girl here."

She nods her head at Charlie in the foyer who hesitantly takes off his coat and hangs it up after getting the not-so-subtle hint from Monroe that they're staying. I can tell by the way Charlie slumps forward that he's wondering if there's something going on between Dr. Lang and me, and for some reason I kind of want him to.

Maybe it'd be easier for him to think of me as a friend that way, or maybe I just want him to be jealous. I'm honestly not sure what my goal is here, but I do know I can't go overboard or Sophia will get the same idea, and I don't want that.

Sophia's obsession with getting male attention started after *Mindy and Missy Hart* ended and she was trying to make a comeback as a teen. She wanted the lead role of a pilot that would eventually become a popular vampire show in the late nineties and early aughts, but she was beat out by a talented soap opera star who went on to become a household name.

After she missed out on that defining role, and then several more, she turned to being *the* party girl in L.A.—a socialite desperate to be seen on the arms of popular male celebrities to stay relevant in Tinseltown.

But after years of being known as a sloppy party girl, even the guys who also partied were being advised by their publicists to avoid her. The age of paparazzi lurking around every corner blew up, and no actor wanted a wild reputation like Sophia Taylor's.

And ever since then, she's had this innate need for male attention to feel complete. She can't be fully confident in herself or her abilities unless she can prove she still has the power to lure the men she wants. It's like she doesn't know who she is without one, and she's afraid to find out.

When Dr. Lang shakes Monroe's hand, he acts as if she's just like any other person. "Of course, Ms. Jennings. Lovely to meet you. I'm so glad to hear you've been such a faithful friend to Annette during this difficult time."

That's the thing about Brits, you'd never know if they were starstruck. They always seem to maintain a certain level of poise and control with their fancy accents and polite manners. Monroe and I are accustomed to people who cry, scream, wail, or even faint when they see us in person.

It was alarming at first when people were losing their minds over our presence on a daily basis, but eventually we grew accustomed and better equipped for it. But it's still like a breath of fresh air any time we meet someone who treats us normally, even though they know who we are.

"Yes, she *has* been faithful to Annette. Unlike when I overdosed, and Monroe said she thought I'd already died years ago on live TV," Sophia says as she turns to face us next to the now-brewing coffee maker.

Bringing up her past beef with Monroe on camera was a calculated move, and it's making us all feel incredibly awkward. Monroe takes it on the chin, though.

"I did say that. I was young and immature, and it was really wrong of me to do. Like I've said many times already, Sophia, I'm very sorry."

Sophia turns away to get mugs from the cabinet without accepting Monroe's apology, and Dr. Lang struggles to change the subject. "So, what projects do you have coming up, Ms. Jennings?"

Charlie bends down to whisper in my ear as Monroe and Dr. Lang start discussing her current movie. "Can we talk somewhere alone for a second?"

I'm not sure if he means without cameras, without the three of them, or both.

"Sure, I can turn the cameras off in the library if you like?" I whisper back and look to him for clarification.

His face lights up like the answer was *all of the above*. "That'd be perfect. Want me to wheel you there?"

"Sure," I say, before we sneak off together.

I scroll through my phone and turn the cameras off before we arrive in the foyer. "Okay, they're all off in the library."

"Perfect," Charlie says as he wheels me in and closes the door behind us. He parks me next to one of the wingback chairs and takes a seat on the sofa across from me with his hands clasped together as his legs bounce.

The cameras lights are all red, and I take a deep breath, not knowing what this conversation is going to be about.

"I'm so sorry. If it were up to me, we would've left as soon as we saw you had company. Do you want us to go? Because I'll go grab Monroe in a heartbeat." He looks down at the floor like he can't bring himself to ask me what he really wants to know.

"It's fine, Charlie, really. I mean, don't stay forever because we have work to do, but it's not a big deal to visit. Doctor Lang doesn't have to leave for a while anyway." I smile, trying to reassure him, but now he looks even more uncomfortable.

He shifts in his seat and clears his throat. "Okay. If you say so, then."

"Are you okay?" I ask after I get the sense he's disappointed I didn't offer more information about Spencer and me.

He clears his throat again. "Yeah. It's just going to take some time for me to adjust to the fact that you may eventually move on with someone else. That's all."

"That's not what's going on here. He's an old family friend and my doctor." I laugh trying to ease the tension between us. "You did say you want to be friends with me again, though, and I hope you haven't changed your mind?"

Charlie sighs and forces his legs to hold still. "Even if that's not what's going on right now. Even if it's not with him. It could be eventually ... with someone else. And I guess I never really considered that before today when I walked in and saw your hands together like that. I thought you just wanted to be alone, but now I'm wondering if you just didn't want to spend your time with me."

I rub my temples with my fingers as I try to think of what I want to say and how I want to say it. "I honestly don't know what I want right now. I just know I want to find my new normal," I tell him, feeling more confused every minute about what I'm doing. "And I'd like you to be in it as my friend if you can handle that."

Charlie's eyes start to well up, and he stands to pace the room. "I know. I know. And I do think I can be that for you. I mean ... I know I can. But just know it's hard not to scoop you up, kiss you, and love you like I used to. That's all."

I laugh as tears pool in my eyes. "You can still scoop, you know."

Charlie walks over to my chair and gives me the tightest hug I've had since we were still together. I pet his hair with my hands as we embrace and can't help but inhale his scent even though I've been trying to create distance between us for weeks. But it's in the middle of that tender moment when I notice the camera on the mantel behind him has turned green.

Chapter 9

"Oh no!" I say with a gasp, even though I only meant to think it.

Charlie pulls away from me and looks toward the mantel. "What's wrong? You look like you've seen a ghost."

"I swear I turned those things off!" I raise my voice as I dig for my phone.

"You mean everything we just said was recorded?" Charlie asks, looking betrayed.

"I don't know how this could've happened. I swear I turned them off. I know they were red when we came in."

Charlie sighs and crosses his arms in front of his chest. "I believe you, and I signed on to be filmed anyway. Who else has access to camera control?"

"Just me and Sophia. I guess the crew could've accidentally turned them on, but Frank gave his word they wouldn't."

Charlie goes to the library door and pries it open just enough to hear the conversation between Sophia, Monroe, and Spencer in the kitchen echo throughout the foyer. I wheel over to listen, too, but the only voices conversing are Monroe and Spencer's.

"You know just as well as I do who did this." Charlie narrows his eyes and shuts the door.

"I don't think she would. We can't assume anything. It could've been a glitch or something." I shrug, wishing he'd give her a chance.

"Well, I think you need to let her know her place. Because if she did do it, she's probably done it before, and she'll do it again." Charlie's neck grows red.

I take a deep breath and bite my nails. "Grace made sure I have episode approval, so there shouldn't be any surprises."

"Well, thank God for Grace, because Frank won't have your back at the end of the day. He wants whatever's going to bring in good ratings and advertising dollars just as much as your sister wants fame. For as long as I've known him, his motto's always been *do it now and ask for forgiveness later*. So I wouldn't take him at his word if I were you," Charlie says with a clenched jaw.

"I guess," I agree with a sigh.

"You don't have to do all of this and live with her. I could ..." Charlie throws his arms in the air, then stops himself. "No, I'm sorry, I said I wouldn't go there."

I smile and reach out to clasp one of his hands in mine. "It's okay, I appreciate you looking out for me. I really do."

"The offer still stands. That's all I'm saying," he says as he places his other hand on top of mine and looks me in the eyes for just a second too long, like he wants to say something more, and do something more.

I clear my throat and wheel to the library door. "I'll talk to Sophia about this later, alone. You ready to head back in there?"

Charlie wipes his eyes with a forced smile and sighs. "As I'll ever be."

I hear people talking over me, but I can't wake up. It's like I'm in a never-ending mind fog, and when I open my mouth to speak, no words escape. I try to move my legs, but it's like they're both made of lead. So I'm trapped here with my silent screams forever until a sliver of light comes through the edge of the darkness.

The light grows, and my eyes are now able to open. Mumbling voices around me become clearer, and I want to see who they belong to. I blink a few times until my crusty eyes fixate on Sophia and Dr. Lang, who are studying an envelope. It's the first time I've woken up in my own home after my accident. It's happening all over again ... just how I remember it.

Sophia wears a long face full of hurt and Dr. Lang looks shocked, and I think I might know why. Unlike the last time I dreamt this memory, I can zoom in on the letter that reads *Hush, Dear Sister* written in my handwriting.

I sit straight up in bed and my eyes dart around for Lang and Sophia, but they aren't there. That was an actual memory though, I'm sure of it. It's slowly starting to come back to me. But why would I have written that? If I ask Sophia or Dr. Lang, would either of them tell me the truth, or would they just think I'm crazy?

Photos of Monroe and Charlie leaving my house are all over *TMI* by the time I check my phone later that afternoon. Grace sent me multiple texts with a link letting me know, but as soon as I click on the photos to have a look, she sends a newer link.

Sneak Peek into The Sisters of Crawford Manor, the second one reads. Then a third text from Grace says, *Did you okay all of this? It's already blowing up on social media.*

When I click the last link and the video plays, I think, *Well, no, Grace. Because we only said in the contract—that you helped construct—that I have the right to okay episodes before they air, not trailers.* I'm sure this article is just some basic glimpses into our life and my house or something ... but ... *Oh. My. God!*

I slam my phone down when I realize what's happened and scream Sophia's name without fear of the consequences. Then I turn the cameras off in my room and wait for her.

"What is it? What's wrong?" she screams from upstairs as she makes her way down the steps in a hurry.

"Are you hurt?" She has genuine concern written all over her face as she enters my room, and I'm having a hard time containing my anger.

"Mentally, emotionally? Yes. I *am* hurt." I glare toward her figure in the doorway and catch her eyeing the cameras in my room to see if they're on or off.

"Well, let's hear it, then. What's going on?" she asks with an innocent look on her face.

"This morning, when Charlie and I went into the library to talk, I turned the cameras off. But somehow they were turned back on once we started talking." I tilt my head with a stern expression and wait for her to fill in the blanks.

Sophia sits into her hip and raises her brows. "Well, I certainly hope you aren't insinuating I turned them on," she says as her own temper begins to flare.

"Well, how do you explain it, if it wasn't you, Sophia?"

She steps forward until she's against my bed, where she bends over to look me in the eyes.

"I didn't do it, Annette," she says with a conviction I can't deny. Then her demeanor completely changes when she raises her body upright and catches her own reflection in the wall mirror.

"It was probably Frank! That silly old goat will do anything for a juicy scene." She laughs and fluffs her hair as she studies herself. "Why are you so mad about it anyway? They'll cut it out of the show if you throw a big enough fit."

"Not now, they won't!" I rub my temples and take a deep breath as I browse through social media.

"Why not?"

"Because they just put out an early teaser trailer and have a clip from our conversation in it! It's already getting a ton of buzz all over the internet because people want to know what happens with me and Charlie."

Grace was right, it's blowing up. I already found plenty of theory posts about Charlie and me on Facebook, TikTok, and Instagram. There's no way they won't put it in the show when they've already put it out there as an engrossing preview.

Maybe I shouldn't have done the show if I can't take the heat. I feel like it's already becoming more of a trashy reality TV show than the thoughtful documentary I was promised, and the turnaround time is certainly quicker than I thought it would be, too.

Sophia's eyes widen as she turns back to the mirror with a *better you than me* expression. "Sounds like you're in a pickle then, huh? But what's the big deal at the end of the day? People will see into your love life a little more than you anticipated ... Big deal."

I toss my arms up. "Big deal? It *is* a big deal, because it's not just me they're throwing out there to the wolves to be criticized. It's Charlie, too! And he didn't sign up for that level of exposure. He trusted me."

Anyone that knows Charlie even a little bit knows he stays behind the camera for a reason. He hates that kind of attention. And even though he did sign on as a guest, he's being pitched as a main character based on the trailer.

"But isn't it better that people hear whatever you two had to say to each other for themselves rather than assume he's hooking up with Monroe behind your back like the tabloids have been saying?"

I stop to think of a rebuttal, then realize she has a point. "Maybe, but that's not the point. It was a breach of trust, whether it helps Charlie's reputation in the end or not, and no one should have that kind of power over us and our privacy."

It's then I decide whoever turned that camera on needs to be let go from Frank's staff. End of story. Or I'm done. And I'm going to get to the bottom of it.

"What do you mean it was a breach of trust?" Frank says with his smooth, southern accent.

"That was a private conversation I went to the trouble of turning the cameras off for, and now it's out there as not only a preview to our show, but as a part of an episode you'll now be forced to air. An episode I should've had final approval on according to my contract. But now that approval is shot to hell over a strategic technicality, and I don't appreciate it. Maybe this whole show thing was a huge mistake on my part."

I take a deep breath after my rant and try my best to speak rationally. After all, I haven't even given Frank a chance to defend himself or his team yet. However, my fear of similar things continuing to happen over the course of filming the show has me filled with anxiety. It's one thing to feel bullied or misled myself, but it's a whole other thing when someone tries to screw over someone I love.

"Annette, our team didn't turn that camera on. If you turned it off, they didn't turn it back on, I guarantee you. I'm going to go check on the situation myself to make certain, but I know they would never do that," Frank says with all the smooth, southern assurance he can blow through the phone at me. But no amount of southern charm is going to sweep this problem under the rug.

"You go check with them and get back to me. Because I don't want this to be a thing that happens more than once, or I'm out. Charlie signed on to be an occasional guest star, not trailer bait," I add, with little patience left.

"I'll let you know what I find out, honey. But don't worry. This won't happen again," Frank says before hanging up.

Sophia left to have dinner with Frank. I canceled because I'm not ready to go out and end up in the tabloids again, plus I'm still mad about what happened earlier even though both Sophia and Frank swear it wasn't either of them, or Frank's team.

I'm cozied up on the couch downstairs with a blanket about to watch a romcom when the buzzer for the gate goes off. I planned on lying here basking in my misery all evening, but now I'm going to have to deal with people.

"Can I help you?" I ask with apprehension, expecting excited fans who've discovered where I live, a reporter, or some paparazzi.

"It's me, again. My last two appointments were cancelled, and I thought I'd drop by and see how you were doing. I hope that's okay," Dr. Lang says with a cheerful tone.

I smile with delight that it isn't someone poking around my house as they secretly try to get photos of me in my wheelchair to sell to the tabloids, and I guess it wouldn't be terrible to have company.

"Of course, it's alright. Come on in."

As his car pulls in the driveway, I find myself fixing my hair and throwing on lip gloss. Was Charlie onto something? Does Dr. Lang have some sort of feelings for me, or I for him?

I laugh at how ridiculous it is to consider for even a second. Dr. Lang is like family. I simply take pride in my appearance like everyone else, and just because I don't want to look like a complete ragamuffin in front of Dr. Lang doesn't mean I want to jump his bones or fall deeply in love with him.

The brand-new grandfather clock Sophia surprised me with earlier today strikes six as Spencer walks up the sidewalk and knocks on the stained-glass door. But as soon as I swing it open, I'm suddenly aware that all the cameras are still on inside the house and wonder if he's put that together. Sophia's going to be bummed when she discovers Dr. Lang was here and she missed out on an opportunity to flirt.

Dr. Lang walks in, takes one look at me in my sweats with my blanket in my lap, and decides not to take his jacket off after all. Instead, he grabs mine from the coat rack by the door and motions me toward the back of the house.

"We're going for a walk. Doctor's orders. The change of scenery and fresh autumn air should do you some good. I'll push."

Luckily, I have a sidewalk throughout the back of my property that weaves through a gazebo, a fountain, several ivy-laden patios, and loads of overgrown landscaping I wish I could say Charlie and I were able to tend to ourselves when he lived here with me. We always hired professionals to make this vast space beautiful, but lately I've fallen behind on getting someone to keep it up.

My closest neighbor, old man Godfrey, lives on the other side of a large, wooded area, and sometimes if the tree limbs are bare enough, I can see the lights from his house if they're on. Otherwise, there are no other visible homes.

"It's beautiful back here. Do you take a stroll often?" Dr. Lang pushes me past the maple, willow, and oak trees spread throughout the yard and sucks in a deep breath.

I hesitate before answering, not wanting to remind myself of why I hardly leave the house anymore. "I used to. But since the accident, I … I feel like I just want to be inside."

"And why do you think that is?" Dr. Lang bends to speak in my ear.

I laugh nervously, avoiding a real answer. "I knew you were going to ask that."

Dr. Lang stops pushing and comes around to face me. "Now what did I tell you about calling me Doctor Lang?"

"It's so weird for me to call you Spencer, though." I roll my eyes and laugh.

"New things only seem weird because you aren't used to them yet. But after you get used to them, they're the new normal. So, call me Spencer and get out of the house more often. Breathe in fresh air, lay eyes on the sunshine, and take in this gorgeous land. It'll be good for you." He crouches down in front of me and places his hands on my knees.

I scratch my forehead and force words out that taste wrong. "Alright, *Spencer*, I think I can try.

"See, now was that so hard?" he smiles and stands behind me again, then we change directions and stroll back toward the house.

Spencer is still talking about sunlight and vitamin D, but I tune him out when I catch a figure moving past one of the attic windows. I squint my eyes to focus better, but my heart begins to race with the notion that someone or something is up there.

Spencer wheels me along the path, oblivious to the figure as my adrenaline starts pumping. I see someone up there as plain as day, and Spencer *should* be able to as well.

"Do you see that in the attic?" I ask, slightly out of breath, yet Spencer seems perfectly calm as he finishes his sentence about organic vitamin supplements.

He stops wheeling me and puts his glasses on before looking toward the attic where a figure still stands in the window. "I see the window facing us, yes," he says with confidence as he studies the area.

"What else did you see?" he asks with concern in his voice, and it's then that I realize he doesn't see whoever is up there staring at us, and he probably never will. And if I keep talking about it like this, he's going to think I'm nuts.

When I squeeze my eyes shut and look again, the figure's gone, and so are any hopes I had of ever figuring out what's going on up there.

"Never mind. I think it was just a bird or something," I lie, wondering if there's such a thing as a ghost only certain people can see and hear. But why it would choose me?

My phone starts to ring in my pocket just as I imagine the ghost leaning down to whisper to me while I'm sleeping in my bed alone tonight, and my whole body shivers.

"It's Monroe," I say, and then hit accept with now trembling hands.

"Hey, what's going on?" I say, thinking it's odd she's calling in the evening when she's usually shooting. When I hear her labored breathing on the other end, I grow even more concerned.

"Monroe, is everything okay?" I raise my voice and start to panic even more than I already was.

She takes a deep but shaky breath on the other end of the line before she speaks, as if to gather herself and her emotions.

"I'm okay. Whatever you hear ... I'm okay," she says, then starts to cry.

"Monroe, where are you? What's going on?" I almost feel like I can jump out of my wheelchair and run to wherever she is, injuries be damned. I've never heard Monroe like this, ever.

"Someone tried to attack me tonight when I was getting out of my van at the liquor store over in Gray Hills after shooting. But Big Joe, he ... he stepped in before they could, and they ..."

She starts to cry again and forces a calm breath. "They hit Joe really hard in the head with a bat or something instead of me, and he ..."

But she starts to sob and can't finish her sentence.

"Oh my God, is he okay?" I ask, afraid she's going to say he's dead.

Monroe clears her throat and tries to form words. "He's in the hospital with a severe concussion, but they think he's going to be okay. The person got away that did it, though, and rumors are going to swirl that I was hurt because technically I was in the ambulance with him on the way here. You know how all that goes. People twist things for attention," she warns, and I know exactly what she means.

The media likes to create clickbait headlines like *Monroe Jennings Rushed to the Hospital After Red-Carpet Killer Attack*, just to make people read the article when they knew all along that she was just a passenger in the ambulance. The real victim was someone else the whole time, and they just wanted to make money at their expense. When I think about it, the whole business makes me sick. Don't they ever stop to think what these people's friends and family think when they read headlines like that?

"Do you need me to come to the hospital with you?" I offer, and Spencer furrows his brows wondering what I'm talking about since I'm not talking on speakerphone.

"No, no, no. But, Annette, be careful. I can't believe this is happening to so many of us," she cries, sounding genuinely freaked out, and Monroe never sounds freaked out.

"I worry about you not being able to get around with this psycho killer on the loose. So just do me a favor and be careful. Okay? I've got to go call the rest of my family, but I wanted you to know first. I love you."

"I love you, too, and I'll be careful. Doctor Lang is here with me right now, so I'm not alone," I explain before we get off the phone.

When I hang up, I lean over the side of my chair and start to gag, feeling like I might be sick to my stomach. I suddenly feel nauseated and sweaty thinking about all that just happened to Monroe, and how close she just came to being murdered like the others. Then another wave of adrenaline washes over me, and I aggressively throw up on the sidewalk as Spencer holds my hair back.

"What happened?" He hands me a tissue from his pocket to wipe my mouth on.

"Please wheel me back inside the house," I say with a croaky voice as I cough and cry at the same time, wanting only to be back in my house, back where it's presumably safe.

Chapter 10

My window is cracked, and the sound of the rain outside makes me want to take a nap since I didn't sleep well overnight. I turn all the cameras off in my bedroom and try to lay my phone on the bedside table, but miss, and it plummets to the floor with a thud. I roll over, shut my eyes, and decide to leave it, not expecting anyone to need me in the next few hours anyway since Sophia just left for the grocery store.

After what happened to Monroe last night, Sophia wore a blonde wig and drove my car instead of hers, scared to death that the actress killer might be after her next. I get it, too, because after seeing the figure in the attic and hearing about Monroe's close call, I feel the need to shut and lock my bedroom door any time I'm here alone. And the last thing I want to do is get on my phone or watch TV. No matter where I look, or where I go, all anyone is talking about is the Red-Carpet Killer.

Knowing everything's locked and all the cameras are recording, I begin to drift off into a peaceful sleep where I dream about a sweet little spot on the beach in L.A. that Charlie and I used to go to, and it's almost exactly as it was in real life.

People are roller skating down the sidewalks, the Ferris wheel's spinning by the water, and the sandy beach is glistening where the two of us share a towel and watch families play frisbee. Only when I take a sip of the drink in my hand, I notice that even though Charlie's drinking a cold beer, I'm drinking a sparkling water.

Then, I feel something I've never experienced in real life before. A kick from inside me. Charlie rubs my basketball-sized stomach with a surprised expression on his face. "Ooh. I felt that one."

I smile back at him, filled with more joy than I've ever felt, but then I notice the sky behind him. Everything is suddenly dark, and all the other people have vanished. We're now sitting all alone on the beach in deafening silence.

The ocean's waves are still, the Ferris wheel has stopped spinning, and nothing moves. It's not a peaceful kind of quiet either—it's eerie. I stand and turn in all directions, trying to find someone else, anyone else, but there's no one. Then I wake up to the deafening sound of silence in real life.

All my lamps have been turned off, the TV I left on for low background noise has a blackened screen, and the hum of the heater is silent. The power's out. *Maybe someone hit a power line down the road or something*, I try to reason. But when I sit up in my bed and crane my neck to see out the window past the drizzling rain, I notice that old man Godfrey's house is still lit up even though we're on the same power grid. *This doesn't make any sense.*

A sense of uneasiness rushes through my tingling body as I stare at my doorknob across the room, just waiting for it to turn. Scratching noises on the walls upstairs makes my heart race and skin crawl, and I can't imagine who or what would be trapped in this house unless it were something dark and evil. So I close my eyes and pinch myself, hoping I'll wake up from these inexplicable sounds, that I'm still dreaming somehow. But it doesn't work.

I count to ten while tapping my fingers together like that psychologist on TikTok said to do when you feel panicked. Then I open my eyes to darkness and silence again. It was probably just a squirrel that got in from the rain scratching. I shrug with relief, trying to convince myself all the fuss was for nothing.

But footsteps start to creep down the stairs, and my pulse travels up my chest and into my throat. Sweat builds all over my body, and I struggle to catch my breath knowing I'm not imagining these things, that there's someone else here besides me. Someone living ... or someone dead. And of course, the damn cameras and Wi-Fi are off right along with the power.

I lean across the bed to glance out my window, hoping to see Sophia driving up, but all I see is pouring rain. Mr. Godfrey's house is still lit up next door, close enough to see, but too far to hear me scream for help. Then I picture my phone still on the floor on the other side of the bed and know I should grab it.

I scoot myself to the edge of the mattress and try my best to quietly lower myself to the floor and slide under the bed, but I end up making a ton of noise instead. After the bottom half of my body spills onto the floor with a thud, I crawl under the bed and drag my leg behind me until I reach my phone.

Who should I call, if anyone? I hover over Sophia's and Dr. Lang's names instead of the police, who clearly thought I was crazy last time. Dr. Lang went back to his office about two hours ago and Sophia went to Whole Foods. But Dr. Lang's office is only ten minutes away and the store is about twenty.

I decide to try Sophia first, and maybe by some miracle one of them can get here in time to ward off whoever's here. I spot an old metal towel rack I didn't like and was too lazy to return to Home Goods under the bed, so I scoop it up to use as a potential weapon just in case. I'm not sure who is here or what they want, but I'm not going down without putting up a fight.

Footsteps make their way down the hall with purpose and come closer to my room as I silence my phone with trembling hands. I manage to text Sophia without making any noise, feeling too afraid to call in case her voice is too loud.

Come home right away. Someone's in the house!

I don't hear anything back from her. Then the footsteps pass by my room and go toward the foyer, so I hold my breath. *Wait, maybe they don't even know I'm in here. Maybe they thought I left with Sophia.*

After I don't hear back from Sophia, I decide to text Dr. Lang who answers almost immediately.

Do you want me to call the police? I'm only about ten minutes away from you. Leaving now. Is Sophia not home?

No police. I don't want the media hoopla. Police thought I was crazy last time. Bedroom door is locked. Don't think they can get in. They're just roaming around the house.

I text back with trembling fingers, realizing how strange this whole terrifying thing probably sounds to him. Especially the fact that I don't want the police to come. The truth is, none of it makes any sense to me either. Who would stay in someone's attic and only come out to wander around every once in a while? No one. Because nobody could live like that. Not unless they were already dead.

Stay put and stay quiet. Silence your phone.

I did.

I feel a tiny bit better knowing Spencer's on his way. He's not just my doctor, he's also my friend. A friend I can count on and feel safe with who feels like family.

The footsteps disappear once they reach the kitchen, but I continue to lie in silence under the bed. After a few more minutes of no new sounds, I wonder if they walked out the kitchen door and left. If it was some squatter hiding in our attic while it rained, maybe they booked it out the kitchen door into the driveway and escaped.

I almost have myself convinced that's what happened until the power comes back on then continuously switches on and off like it's possessed. As if something sinister is making it do so to drive me insane.

The constant flickering of lights sends me into a full-fledged panic attack I can't control, and I feel like I'm going to die. My entire body sweats profusely as I gasp for a deep breath I can't seem to suck in while my hands shake uncontrollably—but all I can do is wait in horror for it to end. And as I wait, I'm convinced the madness of it *is* making me go crazy with paralyzing fear.

The constant back and forth of lights on and lights off finally stops after what seems like an eternity of torture, but as soon as it does, footsteps begin stomping around upstairs again. With tears streaming down my face, I cover my ears and hum as loudly as I can to drown out their echo even though I know I'm already being driven mad.

I can't regulate my breathing anymore, and I fear I'm starting to hyperventilate. So I count down from thirty out loud to steady my irrational breathing and block out my terrifying surroundings. *What could they possibly want from me? To scare me out of my home? And why would anyone want me to leave this place so desperately?*

Suddenly, the vibrations of footsteps are replaced with loud music that plays from an old antique stereo I planned to refurbish in the attic, and not even my humming can drown out its off-key melody. An old, classical tune full of distorted notes makes my whole body shiver as a puddle of tears forms on the hardwood floor beneath my chin.

Not even death could be as bad as this terror, and in these enduring moments, I start to think I'd rather be dead than feel this afraid and irrational all the time. I think I hear a car door slam outside my window, and when I completely uncover my ears to make sure that's what it was, I discover a newfound deafening silence in my now seemingly normal house. The front door opens and shuts a few seconds later, and I hear Spencer call for me.

"Annette! Are you still here? Are you okay?"

I can't form words or believe what I'm hearing, but I begin to crawl out from underneath the bed when I hear the familiar hum of the heater. The power is back on. I'm crying uncontrollably now, with relief, trauma, and disbelief, and I can't stop my body from involuntarily convulsing on the floor beside my bed. Spencer enters my room after breaking the vintage doorknob with a powerful kick and gasps in horror when he catches sight of me.

"Oh my God! Did someone harm you, Annette? What happened?" he asks, a little more panicked than I'd expect him to be.

I manage to muster some coherent words after a deep but shaky breath. "Someone was here, the power went out, there was music in the attic, and ... I ... I."

I can't finish because I'm bawling again, feeling even more tortured by the fact that no one is going to believe me this time either.

Sophia enters the house with a sense of urgency, then slams the door shut and locks it. "Somebody tried to run me off the road," she sobs.

Spencer yells toward the kitchen, "I'm in here with Annette, Sophia. You need to come right away."

Sophia races toward my room in tears. "She didn't do it again, did she?" She grabs her chest when she sees me and takes in a long breath. "Oh, thank God. She's okay."

"I didn't do what again?" I ask Spencer, and he looks over at Sophia with raised brows and then back at me.

"Someone tried to run you off the road?" He stands and touches her shoulder with concern as she covers her mouth with her hand and wails.

"Yes, some crazy person tried to run me off the cliff on eighty-seven on my way to the store. Probably the Red-Carpet Killer! It was raining, and they ... they tried to kill me! Another car pulled up behind them and saw everything, though, so they took off," she says as tears stream down her distressed face. "They called the police and stayed with me on the side of the road until they came and made a report."

"Oh my God, Sophia. I'm glad you're okay. Thank God for that other car!" I try to process all that's happened to the both of us, but then it dawns on me what Spencer just said to her when she came in and how it doesn't make any sense.

"Wait. What did you mean before? I didn't do *what* again? You don't believe me, do you? I swear there was someone in this house besides me! And if the power hadn't gone out, then it would've been on camera," I say between cries of my own.

"Someone was here, too? Then there's two of them?" Sophia asks, confused as she wipes her tears with a tissue.

"Listen, Doctor Lang, maybe we should tell her about the letter." She shrugs in defeat with a shaky voice.

"She's different now ... and in a better place. Don't you think she deserves to know?"

A scowl grows on my face as Dr. Lang hangs his head in defeat.

"Go get it," he says with a sigh, then Sophia goes to retrieve something upstairs.

"What is going on? What don't I know? Why does this stuff keep happening to me and then no one believes me afterward?" I yell with frustration, wondering why I'm always the one in the dark in my own home.

Spencer grabs my hand. "No one said they didn't believe you. I believe *you* believe what you're saying, even if it isn't exactly what happened. I'm just, I'm not sure that we can count on your ... Well, it's got to do with why Sophia was so scared when she came in here. She thought you might have tried to hurt yourself again."

"When have I *ever* tried to hurt myself?" I ask, genuinely not understanding where he's going with all of this. *Do they honestly think I'm trying to drive myself crazy?*

"When I first found out about the night of your accident, I thought what everyone else thought ... that a burglar must have done something to you. Advertently or inadvertently."

He pauses and looks over his shoulder for Sophia. "But then, when we got you home from the hospital, we found the note."

"A note? A note from who? The serial killer?"

"Well, that's what we'd like to ask you, actually." Sophia enters the room again with an envelope in her hand. An envelope just like the one I've been dreaming about and having visions of.

Sophia pulls a letter out of the envelope and shows it to me. "It's a goodbye letter."

She wipes away fresh tears running down her cheeks. "A suicide note." And on the front of the envelope it reads *Hush, Dear Sister*, in my handwriting.

Chapter 11

Hush, Dear Sister, just like the song Sophia used to sing to me when we were kids and I was scared. It does kind of seem like something I'd put on a note like this if I ever wrote one. But there's no way I'd ever actually do it. Not in a million years or under the worst of circumstances.

The evening of my accident is still blurry and incomplete in my tangled mind, but I do remember what happened earlier that day with *some* clarity.

THE DAY OF THE ACCIDENT

I roll over to the sun shining brightly in my bedroom window, but when I reach over to Charlie's side of the bed, it's cold. For a second, I forgot all about him leaving yesterday morning after our huge fight, but now the terrible memories all come crashing back into my groggy mind.

He's all the way at Eric's in Scottsdale now, and I don't know that he'll ever be in this house again, let alone my bed. He's only been gone for one day, but the gaping hole our broken relationship has left in my heart makes it feel like it's been months since I've seen his face or felt his touch.

I still can't believe it's come to this after all we've been through. We both feel like this is more of a break than a breakup, but it might end up being permanent if he can't support my decision to get back in touch with the only family I have left.

He *should* understand, especially since he went straight to his brother's house in his time of need. I realize Sophia's far from perfect, but since my parents died, I've felt the need to reach out to her in hopes of building back some kind of relationship. Monroe clearly agrees, and doesn't want her back in my life either, but the difference between them is that Monroe's willing to tolerate Sophia to an extent. She's willing to try and make it doable for my sake, at least.

Charlie, however, says he isn't willing to budge, and he doesn't think it's wise for me to let her back in because it's going to be the same story all over again. She'll fall off the wagon and blame me and Charlie for everything just like she did years ago.

I hope one day he may reconsider giving Sophia a chance for me, but since I've been distant, depressed, and confused this past year, I fear his patience has worn thin with me as well. Losing my parents has broken me down, and my grief has transformed me into an entirely different person. Neither one of us saw any of this coming, and we don't know how to handle all the challenges it's brought either.

I hardly recognize my own face as I wipe fresh tears from my eyes because they're so swollen. I guess crying for a whole day nonstop will do that. My phone vibrates on my nightstand, further bringing me back into reality.

I'm so sorry. I have a late call time for re-shoots at 6 now, so I won't make dinner at your house. Are you doing okay after yesterday? I'm so sorry about Charlie, I just know you two will work things out. I'll pop by as soon as I'm done. Love you.

I sigh with disappointment and text Monroe back that I understand, because I do. I've chosen to slow down on the work front this past year, which may or may not have been a wise decision. I wanted so badly to just sit back and enjoy my life with Charlie after I mourned the loss of my parents, only to learn that my on-going grief hasn't allowed that to happen like I thought it would.

Acting is something I love, but sometimes I feel like I'm missing out on my own life and feelings by only ever living out someone else's. Contrary to popular belief, being an actor requires a lot of work hours, and they aren't set hours like a typical nine-to-five job where you can compartmentalize your work from your own life in the evenings.

Taking on a deep, draining role will undoubtedly get me in a funk, so I figured my grief-stricken home life would similarly bring down my mood at work. I wanted to ensure I felt all the emotions of losing my parents without stifling them for work's sake, so I took the time to make sure that everything was properly dealt with. What I didn't know is how strongly my mourning would affect me, and that it might've been healthier for me to go to work and not think about my loss every waking second.

I'm not complaining about acting because I love my job and I feel so blessed that I get to be creative every day. But reshoots are often all-nighters, and even when you're done filming and things have been edited, there are tons of promotional events and interviews to attend once things are all said and done. It wouldn't be bad if I could just talk about my work and promote it. But that won't fly this day and age.

The public has grown accustomed to more from actors, especially women. They feel entitled to know every single aspect of our personal lives as well as our professional ones because they know us on some level. *That level* being us acting like made-up characters, which ironically means they don't know us at all.

I avoid thinking about my parents' last moments because that's not how anybody wants to be remembered, and it's not something I'm open to being asked about during promotional interviews, which would undoubtedly happen. There's always that one interviewer who wants to ask the question your publicist specifically told them not to, and then you look like a jerk if you call them on it.

After an afternoon spent crying on the couch and forcing myself not to call or text Charlie, I decide to veg out alone and watch an old Hitchcock film they're playing on TCM. The last thing I want to watch is a romcom, that'll just push me over the edge. I might as well put Charlie's ring back on my finger and forget about Sophia for the rest of my life, because I'll be re-thinking everything we fought about afterward and simply want him back.

I begin to fall asleep on the couch watching *Friends*, having instantly regretted the scary movie decision I made earlier knowing good and well I'd be home alone all night. For some reason, I thought an episode of *Friends* after *Rear Window* would erase any lingering feelings of suspense, but I was wrong. I contemplate sleeping on the couch all night so I can be more aware of my surroundings but ultimately decide that's ridiculous and head to my room like a normal adult.

Sleeping in my bed without Charlie just feels wrong, so I decide to sleep in one of the guest rooms upstairs. I'm halfway up the steps when I think I hear a floorboard creak in the hallway ahead. It came from the corner leading up to the attic, but by the time I reach the top of the stairs and flip the light on, there's nothing there.

Maybe it's the Hitchcock movie playing games with my mind and an old house doing what old houses do, or maybe it's really haunted and I'm just now noticing it now that Charlie's gone. Maybe they only get brave enough to come out when it's me here by myself.

No, now I sound crazy. I laugh as I go into one of the guest rooms and shut the door behind me. I hop into bed, plug my phone into my charger, and pause again when I hear another floorboard creak, only this time it's coming from the attic.

I run and lock the door to my room as my heart rate soars, but I'm still hoping I'm just spooked from watching a scary movie. I mean, I haven't been alone in a long time at night, and this is probably normal. Just a phase I have to go through until I get used to not having anyone else here.

Even when I was little and afraid, Sophia was always there to comfort me. I haven't spoken with her in years now, not *really*, but I've always kept up with her life through Mom.

She always refused to get on the phone and try working things out with me, and eventually Mom stopped telling me about all her stints in rehab because it made me so frustrated that they kept giving her their hard-earned money. It only enabled her further, and then I'd have to fund them because she'd sucked them dry.

I guess they felt like they owed it to her after she was the breadwinner in our house for years as a child star, but doing the same thing over and over and expecting different results is insanity. And the three of them lived in insanity with each other for a long time.

Any time I went for a visit, Sophia would stay with a friend until I was long gone to avoid any run-ins. For some reason, hating me and my success from afar made taking my money easier for her. Plus, she hated that I was still with Charlie.

Feeling down about Charlie and depressed about my nonexistent relationship with my sister, I find a pen and a piece of paper in my guestroom's nightstand and start to write a note to her in an attempt to forget about my fears. I miss my parents beyond belief, and I know she's the only other person who could understand my pain right now.

I write the words *Hush, Dear Sister*, knowing she'll get the old reference, only I can't seem find the rest of my words. How do you reconcile with someone after so many years of not speaking?

I grab my glass of water on the nightstand, take a sip, and go to the bathroom down the hall to wash up before trying to finish my letter. But that's the last thing I remember ...

As the story goes, Monroe held up her end of our bargain for a much-needed *girls' night in* at my place after she finished working on set. She ended up dropping by later that evening only to find an open gate and an unlocked front door. When she apprehensively stepped inside, she found me unconscious at the bottom of the stairs folded up into a position so terrible she assumed I was dead.

The police grabbed prints off of a light switch in my room and found that my jewelry box had been tampered with and stolen from. They arrested Thomas Nichols a few weeks later after he hit a house down the road and his prints matched the ones on the light switch.

Only he still claims I'd already fallen down the steps when he entered the unlocked house, and when saw me lying on the floor he thought I was dead, so he took what he could and got out. He also claims he received an anonymous tip from a burner phone telling him my house would be up for grabs that night, and that's what prompted him to come in the first place. That he was tricked into being a scapegoat.

As for me, I only remember waking up in the hospital the next day with Charlie and Monroe by my side. And I'll never forget the way we all cried when they told me about my condition. How the nerve damage could be temporary but might be permanent. It was like grieving my parents all over again in a way, because the future I thought I had to look forward to was gone.

All I could think about was how this would ruin Charlie's life as well if he were to get on board with the Sophia stuff like I'd wanted him to. All his hopes and dreams for a brilliant writing career, traveling, being active, and having a big family would crash and burn in that bed right along with me and my failed plans just because he loved me.

I knew I didn't want him to go down with my ship. I couldn't do that to him—even if he did eventually come around to Sophia. So I pushed him away, *hard*.

As I look at the note I supposedly wrote before somehow hurting myself, I can't believe what I'm seeing. It *is* my handwriting. But it can't be, because as bad as things had gotten, I wouldn't have done this to myself. And if Thomas Nichols is telling the truth, it doesn't explain his anonymous tip.

I look at Sophia and Spencer and shake my head. "I was okay that day. Not perfect by any stretch of the imagination, but okay. I really was. I just don't see how this could've happened," I say with tears of doubt and confusion streaming down my face as they look at me with pity.

"Maybe that Thomas Nichols guy wrote this? Or he forced me to." I suggest, knowing it's a long shot.

Sophia rushes to my side as Spencer pats my hand. "I'm sorry, Annette. I thought you deserved to know. Perhaps you just weren't in your right mind that night after the breakup."

I glance toward the corner of the room and notice that the cameras are on, and not only did it seem I was not in my right mind on the night of my accident, it sure as hell looks like I'm not in my right mind now either. The cameras will show nothing strange happening in the house that led to my absurd behavior. No intruder, no creaking floors, no music playing from the attic ... only me acting hysterical for no apparent reason.

I take a long, hard look at myself and my behavior lately, and suddenly find myself questioning everything. Maybe my mind isn't reliable because I'm dealing with PTSD, trauma, or I'm having a psychotic break?

"Maybe you should take something for your nerves and just try to rest for a while. We can finish talking about this once you're calm and well-rested. And perhaps this is something she won't want to be filmed, Sophia." Dr. Lang turns to her with a compassionate smile after he notices me eyeing the green-lit cameras in the room.

"Oh, God. I need to make sure this gets cut from the show. I don't want anyone to see this note and think I wrote it," I cry as Spencer helps me into bed and tucks me in like a child.

"I'll talk to Frank," Sophia promises.

"And I'll be here when you wake up. I'm not going to go anywhere. Okay?" Spencer hands me a pill and some water.

After they both leave my room and head into the foyer, I'm left alone with my paranoid thoughts of what's going to happen next. I reach into my nightstand drawer, take another anxiety pill, and close my eyes. I don't think a restful sleep is in my near future even with the pills, but being awake all night will mean I've got a lot of time to go over what's happened, who I trust, and most importantly, whether I trust myself.

Chapter 12

Yesterday completely wore me out. I feel like I've been in a year-long coma when I wake just after nine and finally read Monroe's text from last night.

I'm coming to get you in the morning for a day out of that house. I could use a break too after what happened. Be there at ten thirty. Dress comfortably.

God, if she only knew what happened here yesterday, she probably would've come here guns blazing insisting on spending the night here with me, and I must admit, I'm looking forward to being with someone who may believe me.

Yes, please. So much to share with you. Hope Big Joe is getting better. See you soon.

After I manage to get into my wheelchair, I roll over to my window and notice Dr. Lang's car is still out in the driveway, which means he stayed overnight like he said he would. Almost all the leaves on the sea of trees outside have fallen overnight, and I now have a clear view of old man Godfrey's house. My window feels cold to the touch even though the sky is clear and bright, and I feel like maybe things are starting to look up.

Yesterday felt too heavy for my soul—too dense, too out of control. Reliving those awful events in my head again makes me nauseated and anxious, so I decide to let it go for now and take a refreshing shower to clear my head. On my way into the bathroom, I hear Sophia and Dr. Lang whispering in the foyer, so I wheel to my bedroom door and crack it open to eavesdrop.

I can't tell what they're saying exactly, but I do sense a tone of concern in both of their low voices. I mean, I know he said he would be here when I woke up, but does this mean he stayed because he thinks I'm unstable rather than for emotional support? Do they both consider me a suicidal maniac who's capable of anything? Like I've completely lost my mind.

I decide then and there that I'm not going to act crazy anymore. I don't care if a ghost comes into my room and holds a knife up to my throat, I'm *not* screaming or asking anyone for help. The last thing I want is Sophia thinking I'm incapable of running my estate, my money, or making my own health care decisions.

She could probably put me on a 5150 psychiatric hold with the way they found me yesterday alone. I could potentially lose everything and be committed into a mental institution thanks to my recent odd behavior and that damning suicide note.

But I'm not going to let anything like that happen. I'm just not. Yesterday was the last time I'll allow myself to give in to my irrational fear. After all, nothing *did* happen. The fear of what could potentially happen to me for freaking out over nothing is far worse than seeing the boots standing outside my door yesterday. That person didn't actually *do* anything anyway, except stand there and scare me to death. However, maybe the only reason they *didn't* do anything is because I had my door shut and locked.

My mascara isn't quite dry yet when I hear knocking on the front door, but when I glance at my phone, it says it's only ten o'clock. I guess Monroe came early. I haven't even had time to come out of my room and talk to Dr. Lang and Sophia about yesterday yet, and I desperately need to get a feel for what they're thinking. Sophia isn't going to be happy about me leaving the house with Monroe, especially after her close call on the road yesterday.

Three voices come from the foyer, so I rush to finish my makeup and gather the things I'll need for the day before all hell breaks loose out there without me. By the time I grab my purse, phone, and keys, I already hear Sophia's raised voice echo throughout the house. When I wheel into the hall leading to the foyer, I see the three of them standing there arguing.

They all freeze when I round the corner and look at me like I'm a porcelain doll on the brink of shattering. Monroe gives me a smile before she starts speaking in a calm tone. "She'll be perfectly safe with me. I have security following me at all times now in case I need them."

Dr. Lang nods his head in agreement with Monroe, and Sophia scoffs at the two of them like she thinks they're in cahoots together.

"Whatever." She folds her arms and starts stomping toward the kitchen with a scowl of defeat on her face.

"But we're going to have to talk about yesterday and the note." She turns and says with her hands on her hips, and I look to Monroe with raised brows.

"Let's go," Monroe says as Dr. Lang follows us out the front door, and I wonder if Monroe knows about the note now, too, since she didn't look confused when Sophia mentioned it.

Once I'm in Monroe's van, Spencer leans down to whisper in my ear as Monroe starts the engine, "Listen, I'll try to work on Sophia while you're gone. Call me if you need anything. I'm going to head home soon, but I'll check back in later." He winks and shuts the door.

I smile back, feeling grateful for his support through all of this and for the way he can calm my sister. "Thanks for staying, by the way. I feel bad you thought you needed to. I'm fine now. I-I just, I got a little spooked, that's all"

"We'll talk about it later. Okay? You try to relax and have fun today."

I give him a weak smile as Monroe cranks up the stereo to play an Ed Sheeran song. "I will."

"You knew about the note, too?" I raise my voice once we're out of the driveway and onto the main road by the cliffs where Sophia was almost killed yesterday.

"It wasn't on you that night when I found you. Sophia discovered it upstairs while you were in the hospital. She told us about it the next morning at the hospital, and she refused to share it with the police. She was really freaked out that you would do such a thing ... All of us were."

"Who exactly is *all of us*?" I ask with narrowed eyes, feeling betrayed that no one felt the need to tell me any of this until now.

Monroe sighs. "Charlie, Sophia, and I agreed on something for once in our lives. We all thought it was best to keep the whole suicide note quiet. None of us wanted all of that out in the press for your sake, especially with the mess you were already in. And luckily, there happened to be a burglar to blame for what happened to you, so when the break-in part of the night was solved, the media ran with the assumption that he somehow harmed you in the process."

My eyes widen, and I can't believe they'd let a man go down for attempted murder when all he did was break into a house and steal a few things. "How could you all do that to him? I mean, I know he's a thief but still, that's a lot different than a murderer."

"Listen. It's not how it sounds. In the police report, it says it's *inconclusive*. They didn't know whether you accidentally fell before you were robbed or whether the robber pushed you. No attempted murder charges or assault charges were brought onto him with no solid proof or enough reasonable doubt, so don't worry about him being falsely accused of anything he didn't do."

I rub my forehead and take a deep breath, not being able to process all I'm hearing. "So everyone was in on this 'story' then? Even the police who wrote the report?"

"That's all you need to know, trust me. You still don't remember anything else about the night of your accident, do you?"

I sigh with even more frustration, then lie, "No."

Monroe takes her eyes off of the road to give me a worried glance as she turns her CD off and the radio automatically turns on. "You're not telling me something. What's wrong?"

I start to play with the ends of my hair like I always do when I'm really bothered. "What's wrong? You mean, besides *everything*?"

Monroe turns on her low, calming voice. "I know, I know. Just start with what's bothering you the most."

"Well, I feel like everyone knew this huge secret about me and no one bothered to tell me about it until now, for one. And it's embarrassing that all of you are so sure I did this to myself when I still don't think I would. How did you all get the police to lie like that? It just ... it seems so weird to me that I'd get robbed on the exact same night that I supposedly tried to kill myself. Honestly, none of it makes any sense whatsoever."

Monroe bites her lip. "I don't know what to think, Annette. You and Charlie were so happy before everything just blew up. Or you seemed to be at least ... and I know I can't assume that just because we're best friends that you'd automatically tell me everything, but I think I'd know if you were past your breaking point."

"And what about the anonymous text Thomas Nichols got? Was that from the Red-Carpet Killer?" My heart starts to pound in my chest after saying the name out loud. Was I the first victim in this mess, and he just screwed it up somehow?

"I don't know whether to believe that Nichols guy or not, or what I think about this killer person," she says with a scared look on her face as we turn on the freeway toward the harbor.

I turn to look at her with furrowed brows. "We're going to the harbor?"

Monroe suddenly changes her demeanor and smiles like she's pleased with herself. "We are. Got a fun surprise for you there."

I laugh sarcastically. "Did you become a sailor overnight?"

"No, but you aren't too far off," she says as we continue toward our destination while someone on the radio starts to recap the recent attacks of the Red-Carpet Killer. Apparently, word of Sophia's and Monroe's attacks were both leaked to the media.

Monroe turns the radio off and starts playing her Ed Sheeran CD again as my stomach turns thinking about both of their near misses. After a few more minutes, we turn into the driveway of a quaint cottage tucked inside an inlet. In the backyard there's a visible dock leading to a nice pontoon boat sitting on the beautiful blue water.

"You bought this, didn't you? Oh my God, it's adorable!" I smile from ear to ear and lean forward.

"*I* didn't," she says.

"I'm so confused," I say, but then recognize the car parked at the back of the house. "Oh my God. He did it!" I whisper as tears form behind my eyes.

Monroe puts her van in park at the top of the driveway and comes to help me out. "He did. And he got the pontoon instead of a sailboat. Just for you."

The front door of the house opens as soon as I'm settled in my wheelchair, and Monroe shuts the doors to her van. Charlie walks out the front door and shrugs with a knowing smile as I wheel onto the sidewalk of his beautiful cottage.

"It's so gorgeous here, Charlie! I'm so glad you finally did it!" He runs to give me a hug. "I'm so happy for you."

"It's yours, too, you know." He turns to look at the house and then back to me. "What's mine is yours, really. Any time."

I look past him to take it all in and notice the shiny new ramp leading up to the front porch. When I realize he did do all of this for me, a tear no one sees breaks loose underneath my sunglasses.

Monroe calls to us from the driver's seat of her van as she steps back inside. "It's supposed to be seventy today. You two have fun and call me when you need me to take you back home. Oh, and if anyone asks, we went shopping."

"You sure you don't want to join us?" I look to Charlie for affirmation.

"No, honey. This was my master plan all along. I'm going to visit Big Joe at his place. He went home earlier today. Doing much better now, but he still isn't a hundred percent yet." She frowns.

"My new security is already following me if you didn't already notice." She points at two black SUVs parked two houses down on the street.

"Good! Hey, tell Big Joe I said hello, and give him a big hug for saving my best friend while you're at it," I say as she backs out of the driveway with her window rolled down.

"Will do. Keep her safe, Charlie. I don't want Sophia trying to kill me because you let her get hurt on my supposed watch. She was especially vile today anyway. Annette will fill you in." She rolls up her window and pulls out onto the road, and the dark SUVs follow her.

My hands are clammy as I watch her leave because I'm just now fully realizing that Charlie and I are going to be alone together All. Day. Long. And it's not that I don't want to be alone with him. I do, and *that's* what scares me.

"So … show me around," I say with an upbeat tone, hoping it will give off a platonic vibe as I zoom up the wheelchair ramp that was no doubt specifically built and installed for me. In front of the bonus house we talked about getting together for years. *Our* bonus house.

Charlie skips ahead of me to open the door to the navy blue, board-and-batten house, and when I enter, it's a familiar scene. An open-concept great room featuring a white kitchen and black granite countertops, dark hardwood floors, and linen-covered couches and loveseats that scream hominess.

"It's twenty-four hundred square feet. Two bedrooms, a separate two-car garage, and boat slip in the back."

I look around with wide eyes full of disbelief. "It's beautiful. When did you buy this?" I ask, trying not to address the fact that I totally picked out most of the things laid out in front of me.

"I bought it three weeks ago and had my friend Anderson flip it to my liking. He does great work," he says nonchalantly, as if this isn't the exact bonus-home aesthetic we discussed many times together.

I giggle and feel the need to address the obvious in some way. "Well, you know *I* love it," I finally say as Charlie snorts.

"I guess a part of me was still hoping it could be ours. Eventually. Someday down the road. If you want, I mean." He looks down.

I bypass that entire conversation and decide to wheel toward the bedrooms for a quick look instead. "He did a wonderful job. I couldn't have designed it better myself, honestly. It's picture-perfect."

Awkward silence fills the air around us as we continue down the hallway toward the bedrooms. Charlie keeps looking at me with a longing look in his eyes every time he shows me a new room, but I keep trying to come up with new distractions to prevent us from saying all the words we're thinking.

"Show me the boat," I suggest, wheeling back toward the front door before he can say whatever sentimental thing is on his mind as we tour the master bedroom.

"Actually, we can go out the back. The deck has a ramp, too."

After we exit the back door, I'm fighting tears as I wheel down the ramp from the deck onto the sidewalk leading to the boat. All the hard work and thought he put into this place is really starting to mess with me.

Thinking about it too long makes me want to leap in his arms and hold on for the rest of our lives like we always planned. But is that what's best for him, for me, for us? Are we going to be able to make it through this day without breaking down the walls I've worked so hard to build up between us?

"This part is a little steep. Let me push you to make sure you don't go crashing into the water." Charlie grabs the handles of my chair and guides me toward the crystal-blue waters.

The pontoon is straight ahead, all white with blue trim, the exact opposite of the house. I half expect my name to be written across it in cursive writing, but only the brand name is showing. The sky is clear, and the air is crisp and cool, but the tension between us feels as deep and thick as the water.

"Here we go." Charlie pushes me onto the boat. "She seats about twelve people, and there's a shade cover for when it's warmer. I decided something bigger and more chill would be a better investment long-term."

I smile back at him as I do the translation in my head. He thought something slow and less wobbly would be better for me and more feasible for the kids he still hopes are in our future together.

Only nothing has changed regarding his feelings about Sophia, and I've still got a long way to go to get better, much less to have children. And the last thing I want is him dropping everything in his life to take care of me when we can't even agree on who I'm allowed to have in my life.

He pushes my chair onto a contraption he either made himself or had someone else design that's attached to the floor and the back wall of the pontoon in between the other seats. There's a blank space between them filled with special hardware that can safely secure and lock my chair into place.

"Isn't this amazing? I found blueprints for it online and made it myself a few days ago in case Monroe pulled off getting you here," Charlie says while he starts to lock me into place.

"There's even a seat belt, too." He reaches across my waist and buckles me to the wall with care, but the sudden closeness of our bodies makes my skin tingle. I can't help but inhale the smell of his hair as he bends in front of me to fasten my chair to the floor, and I know this day is going to be a challenge.

When he looks up and asks if I'm comfortable, it's all I can do not to lean forward and press my lips to his. If only my painfully strong feelings for him could be numbed by medications as well, but life's not that simple.

"Thanks, I'm good." I clear my throat, suddenly feeling hot. "You have anything to drink out here?"

He pauses and seemingly looks right through me, as if he knows everything that was just going through my mind because it was going through his, too. Then he stands to his feet and walks toward the front of the boat where he pulls a cooler out of a hidden compartment.

"Seltzer water, wine, beer, or Coke?" I perk up at the idea of playing it safe with seltzer water while simultaneously wanting the wine to loosen me up a bit.

"I'll take one of those little wines and a seltzer," I answer as I tug on my seatbelt, knowing good and well that this is going to be a bumpy ride.

Chapter 13

The water is somehow healing my soul, or maybe it's the entire mini wine bottle I just downed without the accompaniment of my seltzer water that's doing the healing. Either way, I'm feeling more myself today than I have in a while.

However, allowing myself to fall back into my old life with Charlie is not something I want, because I may not be able to recover from a second round of splitting up, and I don't want to lose him completely.

Charlie pulls us into a secluded cove, throws the anchor down, and turns the radio on low. The sun shines on my pallid skin as I take in a deep breath of fresh air and enjoy the view of the rocky cliffs behind us.

Charlie takes a seat adjacent to me and crosses one leg over the other as he cracks open a beer. "So, what has Sophia all bent out of shape today?"

I sigh at the thought of explaining everything that's happened and don't want to exhaust myself by reliving it all when I finally feel at peace. He deserves to know what's going on, and I do need to get it off my chest, but the topic of my sanity is a real buzzkill.

"Something happened to me yesterday at the same time Sophia was attacked on the road, and to make a long story short, I was traumatized. The power went out at the house, I heard footsteps upstairs, I hid under my bed ready to die, and eventually I saw two feet standing outside my bedroom door just waiting for me. There was creepy music playing from the attic after that, and it was all just too much for me."

Charlie's eyebrows almost touch his hairline as he digests all I've said. "Someone was in the house?"

I shrug my shoulders and roll my eyes. "When Doctor Lang and Sophia found me in my room with no evidence of anyone having been there, they couldn't help but think I'd lost it. Oh, and apparently, I'm suicidal, based on some note I supposedly wrote, but you already knew about that ..."

Charlie spits out the beer he'd just taken a sip of and chokes. "They told you about the note?"

I purse my lips together and nod with exasperation. "Yep. Guess everyone knew about it this whole time except me."

"And you still have no recollection of writing it?" he asks with a sense of hope in his voice.

"Not at all!" I reply and throw my hands up in the air with frustration. "Do you honestly think I would've done something like that?" I ask, willing him to say no.

Charlie furrows his brows and shakes his head. "No. Not at all. I always found the whole note thing to be ... off. For lack of a better word. It just ... it never sat well with me because I just can't imagine you ever being in a place to write it. I mean, I guess you could've been because anything is possible and everyone struggles, but I just don't believe it."

"Then how do you explain the fact that it exists in my handwriting?" I take another sip of my water.

Charlie shrugs his shoulders. "I wouldn't put anything past Sophia. She's capable of just about anything. You, of all people, should know that."

I roll my eyes, knowing he'll always go straight to Sophia for blame. "She wouldn't have protected me by keeping it a secret if she had anything to do with it. I mean, she could've done a lot of damage with that note if she wanted to. And what if I *am* crazy, Charlie? Then what?"

Charlie leans forward with his elbows propped on his knees. "Look here. You're not crazy. Crazy people don't sit around worrying about whether they're crazy or not. And besides ... we're all a *little* bit crazy anyway."

"Then how do you explain the things that have been happening to me in the house?"

"No one would blame you for being a little bit off with all you've been through lately. It's bound to affect you. The trauma of losing your parents, our breakup, the accident, living with Sophia again, the threat of this Red-Carpet Killer, and all the medication required for your pain. Of course, you aren't going to be a hundred percent. No one would be under those circumstances."

HUSH, DEAR SISTER

I sigh and really take in the one person's opinion that matters most to me. Knowing Charlie still sees me as the same person I was before is comforting, but it still doesn't explain what's been going on at the house.

"Let me ask you this ... Do you think it's possible that Crawford Manor really is haunted?"

Charlie scoffs then pauses to think for a second. "I really doubt it. Don't you think a presence would've made itself known at least once in all the years I lived there?"

"Is that how it works? Do we honestly know anything about that kind of stuff besides what's made up for the movies?" I ask with a serious tone.

Charlie blinks slowly with a smug grin. "Well, I guess it's not impossible. But I'd say it's highly unlikely. More importantly, don't you think you'd be better off getting Sophia out of there? All these weird occurrences started when she moved in, right? Shouldn't you be more worried about her and her agenda than a ghost?"

I rub my temple, knowing this conversation is already on its way to him wanting to take care of me instead of Sophia.

"Honestly, I know where you're going with this, and I just don't think I can do it ..." I start to say, but Charlie interrupts me.

"No, no, no. Listen, I'm not going to pressure you to stay with me or let me stay with you. I'm just saying, there are other options besides your sister. Annette, she's a whack job! How do you not see that she still hasn't changed? She's the same person she always was. You saw what she did to your clock!" He sets his beer firmly in his cupholder and clenches his jaw.

"No, I get what you're saying, but believe me, she's changed. She's not perfect, but she's better, and we're bonding. But after yesterday, I'm definitely thinking about some changes. Hearing her whispering about me this morning to Doctor Lang made me a little concerned about what she could potentially do if she's living with me and thinks I'm nuts. I mean, I know I'm going through a rough time, but I'm still more than capable of making my own decisions."

Charlie's eyes grow large at this notion. "Listen, I'm serious. If you get the sense that she's trying to take away your power of attorney or force you into a conservatorship, you get on the phone and call me right away because I won't let that happen!"

"I don't think she is, or that she'd be doing it maliciously if she was. I just think the evidence stacked up against me is starting to look pretty bad. And this probably isn't helping me out any." I hold up my empty mini wine bottle.

"Another one?" He laughs and reaches for the cooler.

With a wiggle of my fingers and a smile, I answer, "Just one more."

On the way back to Charlie's cottage, the breeze hits us a little harder as the sun goes down past the cliffside. After our conversation about Sophia and the house, we ended up laughing and reminiscing about all of our good times together, and now I can't help but wonder where this day will leave us.

What are we now? Friends who secretly hang out and casually talk about our past? A past that consists of countless intimate moments we've shared and don't want to let go of or move on from. How is that something two *friends* can nonchalantly discuss without secretly wondering what it'd be like to do it all over again, and do it even better?

Charlie ties the boat up at the slip, pulls out his custom wheelchair ramp, and unlocks me from my spot. While he gathers his things, I wheel my way off the ramp and up the hill toward the house feeling bombarded with thoughts about my old life with Charlie.

"Back door is unlocked if you want to go on in," Charlie yells toward me as he finishes up his duties on the boat.

I give him a thumbs up as I head inside, wondering how complicated it's going to be for me to go to the bathroom here without help. When I wheel down the hall to the first bathroom on my left, I feel a lump in my throat when I notice the assistance bars next to the toilet that I missed on our tour before.

How in the world could I have been so stupid for so long. This man clearly wants to be with me, take care of me, and love me, and that's all I really want as well. So, why am I *really* preventing that from happening?

Is it because I'm protecting him, or because I'm afraid? Afraid I won't be me anymore without my parents and with my sister in my life. Afraid of having to depend on Charlie in a way I've never had to before. I know I've always prided myself on maintaining my independence while in relationships, but is it my pride that needs adjusting?

If he did come back to live with me, where would Sophia go, and what would she do without our show? Will one season of the documentary be enough to redeem her in the eyes of America so she can have her career back, and is there any way Charlie could make a life with me work while allowing her to be a part of it?

After using the bathroom, I take a long, hard look at myself in the mirror and decide that I'm just as much of the problem as everyone else is, and it's time for me to face myself as I am and stop hiding from the pain.

Charlie is relaxed on the sofa looking for a movie to watch on Netflix. "I thought I'd order something in, and we could watch a movie or something. Unless you need to go …" he asks as he points the remote toward the TV and clicks.

"I think that'd be nice. Does that Mexican place off the highway deliver?" I lock my wheelchair into place and pull my legs up.

Charlie jumps up to help me onto the couch, and I let him. "Yeah, they do, actually. I'll order you whatever you like, just let me know what sounds good," he says with excitement in his voice like he can see my guard coming down. After laying a blanket down on the couch next to me, he grabs his phone to look up the menu as I get settled, finally feeling at home for the first time in a long time.

As the movie credits roll and the TV turns dark, I text Monroe that I'd better be getting back, and she responds that she's already on her way.

"I wish you'd stay."

"And I wish things were different." I give Charlie's hand a squeeze.

"They could be ..." He tucks my hair behind my ear and scoots closer. "I'll try to make it work with Sophia if that's what you want."

"You would? You could do that?" I ask, my voice shaking and my bottom lip quivering.

"I still don't trust her, but if having your sister back in your life is what you need, I can do my best to make it easier for you. She and I can coexist. I just needed some time to realize that, and I'm so sorry it took me so long to get here."

Tears well up and sting my burning eyes as my heart soars. "It means the world to me to hear you say that. Truly."

Charlie then leans forward and pulls me into him for a soft kiss that will ultimately turn my entire world upside down.

Chapter 14

That kiss still haunts me when I go to bed the next night. And keeping the fact that we're *back on* from Sophia makes my stomach knot up with guilt. But until I'm sure of how I want to go forward with Charlie and how I'm going to handle Sophia moving out of my house, I can't risk saying anything. Not yet. She'd only assume Charlie's squeezing her out of my life completely.

I turn the lights and cameras off in my room, lay my phone down on my nightstand, and take a deep breath in. But as soon as I get settled, my door creaks open and I see Sophia's frame standing in the light of the hallway. "You forgot your meds."

My heart starts to race as I lift my head up and turn on my bedside lamp. "Oh, right."

Sophia lays all of my medications down with a glass of water on my nightstand, then turns the overhead light back on. "Everything go okay yesterday when you were shopping, because you didn't have much to say when you got home? I mean, I didn't notice any unwanted paparazzi pics online or anything of you all shopping."

I gulp down my pills with one swig of water and hold a finger in the air to let her know I can't respond yet.

Sophia sighs and cocks her head to the side. "Are you still upset about the note and what happened at the house before Monroe picked you up?"

I take another sip of water as I try to think of what I want to say. Choosing my words carefully is important right now.

"I don't want to talk about yesterday anymore. It honestly must've been my mind running away with the sounds of the house settling. So I'd rather just try and forget about it and move on."

Sophia pauses to study me for a second. "Okay," she says with a high pitch, then has a seat on the bed beside me, "but did everything go okay with Monroe?"

I turn my lamp off and lie back down, now facing away from Sophia. Telling her a lie is easier without her studying my facial expressions. "Yeah, it was fun. We got some sweaters and enjoyed the sunny skies," I explain, which isn't a lie. Monroe did pick us up some sweaters after she left me at Charlie's house, and we did both enjoy the good weather, just not together.

"Alright. I just wanted to make sure since you've been so quiet. Goodnight then, I guess." She stands, turns out the overhead light, and leaves with hesitation.

She seems to suspect that something is different, that I'm keeping something from her. But I wonder what she'll do if she figures out that what I did yesterday isn't the only big secret I've been keeping from her. From everyone.

If she knew everything, there's no way she'd be taking care of me right now. And Lord knows I've paid dearly for my sins with the shame and guilt I've carried around since it happened, but sometimes I wonder if that's enough. Maybe that's why I've had such terrible luck this last year. Karma's finally giving me what I deserve.

I nod off and dream of my past life, running free with two legs I could always depend on. Always running from something, or from someone, but I never arrive anywhere or get caught either. It's like I'm stuck in a permanent state of panic getting nowhere.

Diana Rivers and Vera Green are trying to say something to me from the top of a cliff in the distance, but I can't make out their words. Vera's mouth is completely missing from her face as she motions something to me with flailing arms, and I see Diana standing on the cliff's edge as she keeps trying to call me from a rotary phone with a cut cord. In the valley below, I dig in my pockets for my phone, only when I pull it out, it turns into a vial of poison.

I wake up freezing. My room feels like ice, and my bedside lamp is back on along with my TV. I reach for my phone on the nightstand to turn the cameras on, but it's nowhere to be found even though I know I left it there before I fell asleep. I'd swear to it.

My eyes dart around my room knowing I certainly didn't turn the lamp or TV on, and as someone who hates being cold, I'm positive I didn't blast the AC, especially when it's been getting down into the forties at night.

My TV remote sits on the nightstand, so I click it off. The remote for the heating and air conditioning unit lays next to me on the bed, so I crank the heat up to seventy and pull an extra blanket over me from the foot of my bed. The remote reads sixty degrees; no wonder I woke up.

Only with the TV off, I can now hear the scratching sounds from the attic again, so I decide to turn it back on at a lower volume. I leave the lamp on as well and can tell from the way the doorknob's handle is flipped that my door is locked. Thank God Dr. Lang remembered to fix it.

I'm going to ignore the weird things. If I have a ghost, I have a ghost. And if I'm crazy now, then I'm crazy now. No amount of panic and worrying is going to change either scenario, and I don't appear to be in any immediate danger as it is. I mean, what else can I do since no one else can see or hear any of it?

I close my eyes and start to drift back to sleep but hear something I can't discount. "Annette!" my mother's distinct voice whispers, and just like that, I'm taken right back to an uncontrollable state of panic.

I pull a pillow over my head and try to drown the sounds of her voice out. And after a few minutes, I lift the pillow up and take a deep breath when I hear nothing but the low sounds of my TV.

After a few more deep breaths, I turn onto my other side and find my bedroom door is now wide open. The light from my "lost" cell phone flashes on my nightstand, having seemingly reappeared from nowhere, and I'm beyond freaked out.

When I lean toward it to see who the call is coming from, my pulse soars, my throat feels tight, and I scream louder than I ever have before, no longer caring what anyone thinks of me when I read the screen.

Mom calling.

I turn to the other side of my bed where Sophia slept after hearing me scream and see that she's still sound asleep. If she didn't think I was crazy before, she definitely does now. She had to give me a sedative in order to tell her what happened. Then, when she called Dr. Lang in a panic for advice, he said to let me sleep it off and that he'd come by today to check on us.

Maybe I need to leave this house and be done with it. Move in with Charlie and let him take care of me so Sophia won't eventually have me committed for being nuts. Maybe this is how I'm coping with all of the loss I've gone through in the past year, and it's somehow manifested into all these nonexistent things I've created in my mind that seem so real to me. Or maybe I was onto something when I asked Charlie if Crawford Manor really is haunted.

When I grab my phone and open my email, I notice something new from my agent, Grace. The subject line reads *Sisters of Crawford Manor, episode one*, and suddenly I have another theory about the voices in the attic: is it beyond Frank Baxter to make this house seem haunted for better ratings and storylines?

Is he somehow manipulating the cameras, the power, and the "people" creeping around my house for good TV? Something tells me, despite my love for Frank, that I should at least consider it, so I decide to discuss it with Grace.

Without watching the episode, I immediately write Grace back knowing an email won't make it onto camera footage like a phone conversation would. And if for some reason my wild theory proves true in any way, shape, or form, I'm out. Out of this show for good, and maybe out of show business, too, because this isn't worth my sanity.

After I hit send, I take a deep breath hoping that venting to Grace will make me feel better. She won't be quick to assume I'm crazy. She already distrusts Frank, and barely tolerates Sophia, so she'll be open to the fact I may have fallen victim to a vindictive shitshow, even if it *is* ratings gold.

One reason I've always loved and stuck with her as my agent is because she doesn't care about fast money, and she's always kept the long-term images of her clients in mind. She's fierce and loyal, almost to a fault, and I trust her judgment immensely because she's proven she knows how to take care of her clients. And ... she knows how to keep a secret.

"What do you mean, did I have something to do with it? What would I have done? Hire someone to come and scare you for good TV material since there might be a crazy Red-Carpet Killer on the loose?" Frank asks with a surprised tone, then laughs.

"Actually, I *could* see myself doing that, and it's not a bad idea." He ponders the idea, and I can almost see the twisted wheels turning inside his head.

"But I would never do that to you, in all seriousness. And I'm sorry you've been so scared. Do you really think it's haunted?" he asks with a twinge of hope in his voice I can't unhear.

"I don't know, Frank. I'm not sure what to make of all of this." I sigh with genuine frustration because, despite everything, I believe him.

"Well, can you please tell Grace I've got nothing to do with it. She's called eight times threatening to sue me for attempting to drive you insane for good TV." He scoffs then laughs, probably because, deep down, he's glad to talk to Grace for any reason. Even if she's ready to ruin him at a moment's notice for something he didn't do.

"I will."

"Why do you sound so sad I didn't do it?"

I hold my head in my hands and put my phone on speaker. "I guess I was hoping that if you did, at least I'd have some answers."

Frank takes a deep breath and blows it out slowly as he thinks. "Well, tell you what. Let me make some phone calls and see what I can do to help. Then I'll see you later tonight. Hopefully I can help you get some answers *and* provide some good TV at the same time. Deal?"

"Okay? Now I'm really scared," I answer, hoping he knows what he's doing and isn't about to make everything worse.

Dr. Lang's foot shakes back and forth as he sips on his tea. "So, after you gave her the sedative, she was fine, right?"

"Yeah, she calmed down pretty quickly after that." Sophia crosses the room and bites her nails.

"Did you hear or see anything suspicious at all last night?" he asks as she takes a seat across from him on the green wingback chair I bought from the previous owner when I moved in. *God, maybe it's that chair that's haunted, or maybe some other object from the house has a ghost attached to it that I don't know about.*

I remember every piece that was original to the house, and although there are several I kept, much of this place also has my own history stamped all over it as well. The décor, the film history, the secrets it holds.

"I was fast asleep when I heard her scream, and it nearly scared me to death. I didn't hear or see anything strange before or after. Nothing. I mean, except her completely flipping out about Mom calling her."

"Well, I am a bit concerned, Annette," Dr. Lang says as I look at the library cameras that are all lit up green. I guess I did sign up for this, but this is getting to be more and more humiliating as we go.

"I guess the rumors are true and the house is haunted," I say with a half-assed shrug, wanting to save face for the cameras. Having the entire world see me in such a vulnerable state is going to be hard enough without them all questioning my sanity.

"Franks says he's going to be able to get to the bottom of things tonight somehow. So let's not do anything hasty like drug me up on something for crazy people who hallucinate until we see what he has up his sleeve," I say, not fully trusting anyone anymore.

"I was in no way suggesting we throw more medication your way, or that you're mental. I was only going to suggest that we closely monitor you, the situation with the house, and maybe talk about removing some medications if we think they may be inducing anything."

"But per your request, we'll simply put things on hold until we see whatever Frank comes up with. Sophia, are you okay with waiting?" Spencer asks as Sophia flips her hair behind her shoulder.

"Yes. Whatever you think is best, Spencer. I trust your expertise." She crosses her legs the other way, then leans toward him, revealing a hint of cleavage.

I snarl my nose as I watch her flirt, but I don't even notice the face I'm making until she looks at me with furrowed brows.

"Well, good. There we have it, then." I smile and clasp my hands together, knowing I've once again avoided talking about whatever's really going on here. Unfortunately, I also know these two will be questioning my every move from here on out.

As I'm freshening myself up for whatever Frank has in store tonight, I notice my bathroom door won't open all the way. When I pull it back to see what's blocking it, I see an old cardboard box behind it. It feels relatively light when I bump it with the door, so I reach over my chair, lift it onto my lap, and open it with apprehension.

Several items are shoved inside the large box, and I can't imagine what they mean or who would've placed them in here. Maybe Spencer or Sophia found them in storage and threw the box in here thinking I might want to keep them.

I pull out a bottle labeled "paraquat dichloride," a very large knife, a baseball bat, and a Clif Bar. I have no idea what these are or who they belong to, so I shove them back in the box and place it back behind the door.

But then it hits me and my whole body starts to sweat. Somebody tried to hit Monroe with a bat, someone cut Diana's brakes, someone poisoned Vera, and the Clif Bar. Could it be a reference to the cliff Sophia was nearly run off of? Someone's trying to make it look like I did all of this. Like I'm crazy.

I grab my phone thinking I'm probably just being paranoid and decide to google paraquat dichloride. My entire body begins to tremble as I read the words associated with it: *weed killer; banned in several countries; highly toxic to humans; one small accidental sip can be fatal and there is no antidote.*

Panic sets in as the words on my screen blur together and my chest pounds, making me feel faint and nauseated at the same time. I've got to get rid of this before Frank comes here tonight ... But where?

Chapter 15

"Is this a joke?" I ask Frank as a team of people come through the front door behind him wearing uniforms labeled Boo Crew.

Sophia laughs out loud. "Boo Crew? More like *Don't have a clue crew*."

Frank turns to eye Sophia and me, both of us wearing the same skeptical expression. "Their name may be funny, but they're top experts in paranormal investigation. They came prepared with the best gadgets around—voice recorders, night-vision cameras, electromagnetic field detectors, infrared thermometers, binary response devices, and ghost boxes. And if they find something, we can bring someone in to clear the spirit later. These guys are the real deal, y'all," Frank explains as my eyes grow wide with disbelief that this could actually produce some kind of solution to my problems.

"Well, what are we waiting for? Let's see what they can find out. I know I'm curious," I say as we gather at the front door together to watch the rest of the team trail in.

"So ... what are the rules? Can we stay and watch, or do we have to wait outside until they're finished?" I ask as three more Boo Crew members trickle in sporting more paranormal equipment that reminds me of the Ghostbusters.

"We can shadow them as long as we stay quiet and don't interfere. Do you think you two can handle that, because it'd be gold to film it with y'all watching?" He has a twinkle of excitement in his eyes as he huddles the three of us together.

"Are you sure you haven't cooked this ghost story up yourself?" I wince with apprehension as I absorb how happy he seems.

Frank plants his hand over his heart and stands as tall as he can. "I give you my word, my darling. But just because I didn't cook it up doesn't mean I'm an idiot. I know good show material when I see it, after all."

The sun is setting as I drink a cup of tea out on the front porch while Frank and the Boo Crew gather their equipment together inside. I notice old man Godfrey standing in his front yard halfheartedly raking leaves while looking over this way.

I give him a friendly wave back, but he's not looking at me. He seems to be eyeing the crew vans and equipment being brought into the house instead, and I can't help thinking how crazy this all probably looks to him.

Once it's dark out, Frank walks out onto the porch and wheels me inside with a happy dance. "Here we go, babe," he says as we enter an eerily silent house full of people who all turn to stare at us. Frank shuts the squeaky door behind me with a bit too much force, and Sophia jumps.

The man who appears to be in charge walks over to speak in a low whisper, "We're going to start in the attic, where the most activity has supposedly been going on. Please remain quiet no matter what happens. We want the spirits to understand we're friendly and don't want to create any unnecessary trouble."

"Do you normally have trouble?" I ask with a catch of fear in my croaky voice, feeling apprehensive about what we're getting ourselves into.

"Have we ever? Yes. But more often than not, we manage to keep things friendly. Some spirits are naturally aggressive, but if we see that they are, we get out before things escalate," he whispers with confidence. I attempt to swallow away the dryness in my throat, wondering if I'm truly ready to face whatever it is that's invaded my home.

With a lot of effort, Frank and Sophia manage to get me up the stairs leading to the attic despite having no chair lift on that set, and the rest of the crew heads up once we've settled in. Their machines beep as they grow closer, but I'm not certain what any of their sounds indicate.

It could mean they've found something, they're in searching mode, or that they've found nothing at all. Nevertheless, my stomach tightens with every beep, and I find myself clenching my fists with anticipation.

When the experts congregate in one corner of the attic making weird facial expressions at one another, my breathing halts as I wait to learn what they've found. My parents' antique wardrobe is covered by an old, white sheet in the far corner, and they've all surrounded it like it emits something sinister. Frank gives control of my chair to Sophia and urges her to push me forward toward them as he stays back and films us by the exit.

One of the crewmen rips the white sheet off as the others move forward to open the wardrobe doors that barely stand ajar. A man motions the numbers three, two, then one with his fingers as if they're a part of a supernatural SWAT team before he throws both doors open with caution.

A sudden hissing sound makes me jump back in my chair just as Sophia covers her mouth with her hands and takes a step back. With her hands off my chair, I quickly roll down the slanted hardwood floors right toward the wardrobe. With burning hands, I barely brake in front of the wardrobe's doors before a snake slithers out and hurries toward another corner of the attic.

One crewman grabs an old tennis racket lying on top of some boxes and hurries after the snake. He gently picks the creature up and carries it toward the door. Sophia and Frank scatter in opposite directions as the man calmly passes them and takes the terrified snake downstairs.

"It's a harmless black snake. Nothing to be afraid of," he whispers under his breath as he exits, but somehow, knowing it's harmless doesn't make me feel any better about having bunked with it for God knows how long.

"Do you think there are more?" I ask another man as quietly as I can as my body shudders.

"Shhh!" a crewman whisper-yells at me like an irritated Sunday school teacher.

Then another one answers with a kinder tone. "No sign of a nest. Seems to be just the one."

Suddenly, one of the machines goes haywire and emits sounds like a deep but muffled voice while everyone stops dead in their tracks to listen. The words aren't clear, but everyone continues to stand still.

At such a magnified volume it's hard to tell exactly what it is, but the men look at each other as if they recognize what it is and what it said. I back my chair up toward Sophia and Frank, who are now huddled together by the attic door, and try my best to see one of the machine screens showing energies as I pass by a crew member.

The screen looks colorful and wavy when held toward the corner where the secret passageway is, and the man studying it tries to magnify it. I can't tell for sure, but the outline of the colors seems to resemble ... a person.

The noises from the sound machine grow louder and higher in pitch as the man approaches the energy, and suddenly it sounds like a woman's scream growing louder and louder until everything grows silent and dark. The screaming sound. The energy in the corner. Everything is gone.

Everyone continues to roam around the room in search of something, anything, like they're perfectly used to hearing invisible women scream. Every hair on my body stands straight up, and I feel like I could drop dead from a heart attack at any second. I clutch at my racing heart and notice Sophia's face has grown pale as she covers her mouth to stifle a scream.

Frank looks like a leaf could knock him over. He squeezes Sophia in front of him for protection with one hand as he struggles to hold his camera upright with the other trembling hand, then a smile grows on his face when he seemingly realizes he just caught all this frightening action on film. Even though the crew continues to search for more activity, the three of us sense the storm is now over. And as much as I wanted them to figure out what was in the corner, I didn't want anyone to accidentally discover the secret passageway.

If they did, they may follow it all the way down to the entrance outside the library where I hid that big box of evidence someone planted in my bathroom earlier—the one that has my incriminating fingerprints and DNA all over it.

"So, in that moment when you heard those wardrobe doors fling open, what were your first thoughts?" Frank asks Sophia later that night when he decides our show could probably use some in-the-moment interviews as well as some clips of us looking back on events that've already occurred.

Sophia clears her throat and adjusts her hair. "Well, I, for one, expected something evil to leap right out of that wardrobe and attack those men and maybe even us. I'm convinced something dark lives up there now.

"You mean something besides the snake?"

"Yes, something much worse. Probably the thing we've heard scratching around at night and walking throughout the house. And when we heard that awful scream, it just solidified everything," Sophia adds with a flair of dramatic tension.

I look at her like she has three heads, because at no point during my panic attacks about something roaming around the house has she ever mentioned hearing anything herself.

"You've heard things, too?" I turn to Sophia with furrowed brows and put her on the spot as my blood starts to boil.

"Well, I know *you* have, dear. And I've woken up in the middle of the night a time or two thinking I'd just heard a boom or thud or something, but I always just explained it away to myself as a dream or the sound of an old house settling. But after today, after feeling the presence of something in that attic, I think there's something evil living here," she explains, and I can't believe she's suddenly saying she's been hearing things, too.

"And what did you think about today, Annette?" Frank asks as I continue to eye Sophia with a baffled expression.

"Honestly, I don't know. It always seemed, to me, like a person was up there hiding for some reason. I'm still not sure what's going on inside this house, but I'm not convinced that it *is* a ghost *or* that it's not. I mean, the crew left here tonight without finding anything but a snake, technically. So I'm not sure what to make of it all. But that terrifying scream sounded so real, and it scared *me* half to death," I explain, trying my best to be open and honest by sharing what I'm thinking as I'm thinking it.

"That's a perfect place to leave off for tonight, ladies. It still leaves everything hauntingly unsolved. Like a real mystery." Frank stops recording and gathers his belongings.

"You girls sleep tight tonight, and for the love of God, turn the cameras on in your rooms if anything good, I mean *suspicious*, happens."

"Alright. Bye, Frank," Sophia says as she makes a face, shuts the door, and locks it.

I don't know about Sophia, but after tonight, the last thing I want to do is sleep alone. And I'm not sure I fully trust her sleeping right next to me anymore since she clearly lied about hearing things until it was convenient for her and the show. Either she elaborated her story today, or she's been lying all along. It doesn't really matter which one is true, because either way, I've lost trust.

Can you come stay with me tonight? I text Charlie as soon as Sophia goes to her own room, hoping he doesn't think it's an open invitation for sex because I'm honestly not even sure how that would even work for me right now. Honestly, the thought of how it would play out with my injuries is completely mortifying to think about considering how good it used to be.

By the time I've washed my face and brushed my teeth, he texts back that he'll be here in twenty minutes via the secret passageway, so Sophia won't have to know he's here. Not only does the staircase in the walls go from the attic to the library, but it also goes down to the basement and to the back of the house if you keep going.

No one would ever notice the entry door out back from looking at the house because it's covered in ivy, and the old, metal door handle fell off about five years ago. There's an old screwdriver buried in the rocks next to it that Charlie and I have used to open it a few times when we locked ourselves out of the house, but I haven't checked in months to see if it's still there.

Screwdriver still there for the back entrance? he asks.

I haven't checked in eons, have you?

No, but I'll check it out and let you know if it's not there. I'll bring a back-up just in case. See you soon.

He never asked why I even want him to come. I guess he just assumes I'll tell him when he gets here, but the fact that he doesn't even care why and is just glad to come warms my heart.

I've crossed a line now that I've asked him to stay the night with me. A line I can't erase, but I don't care. I need a partner I can trust for whatever is happening here in this house, and maybe not allowing Charlie to be that for me before now is the reason I'm in this position to begin with.

Sophia living here, the show, the odd occurrences in the attic, the killings, none of these things were happening when he was here with me. That accident was a turning point for these strange things, and my whole life changed that day. But did everything in my life need to keep changing after that? Were all of my challenging circumstances exacerbated and made exponentially more difficult because I asked Charlie to leave?

Twenty-five minutes later, I lie in my bed questioning more things as I wait for Charlie. Will he notice and think it's weird that I taped up a huge box and shoved it outside the library entrance of the passageway?

Should I have taken all of my makeup off before he got here so it doesn't seem like I'm trying too hard, and should I be dressed in something other than a giant T-shirt in case we're forced to escape the Red-Carpet Killer or a ghost in the middle of the night?

I don't know why I'm so nervous about him being here. It's not like we're going to be having sex, and Charlie's seen me naked thousands of times before even if we were. But something feels brand new about tonight, and I can't shake the butterflies in my stomach as I lie here impatiently waiting.

Glass bursts into a million pieces in the foyer outside my bedroom, then Sophia curses. The front door opens with its notorious creak, and Sophia giggles as someone else mumbles in a low voice. Another guy?

I guess she didn't want to sleep alone either, which is understandable, but listening to the way she's giggling out there makes me wonder if she's fallen off the wagon again. The two of them tiptoe up the stairs into her room and shut the door, and then it gets quiet.

I check my phone a few minutes later, growing frustrated that Charlie's taking longer than I expected, and I wonder if that back door is giving him trouble. Upstairs, Sophia moans and screams with pleasure as her headboard hits the wall faster and faster while I bury my head in my pillow to drown out their sounds.

After a few more minutes, I uncover my head with a grimace. They've grown quiet again. So quiet, it seems as if Sophia and her man might've left the house altogether. When a car starts and drives off in the driveway, I'm assured I'm right.

As soon as they're gone, the unlocked door to my bedroom creaks opens slowly, revealing a man's shadow in the hallway as my heart skips a beat. "Sorry I'm late. I didn't want to have a run-in with Sophia and her flavor of the week." Charlie walks in sounding out of breath and looking disheveled.

"Are you sure they're gone?" I sigh with relief it's Charlie. "Could you tell who it was with her?"

"Oh yeah, they're gone. I saw them walk out the front door together. Well, he walked, she stumbled. I couldn't tell who it was, but for half a second, I thought it looked like Frank from the back. But there's no way. He'd never stoop so low." Charlie considers, then shakes his head no. "He could never stand Sophia. There's no way. Must've been some guy with a similar build, that's all. Probably some fan of hers we'll never see again."

I nod in agreement with a disappointed frown because it's probably true. She does like to love them and leave them. Historically, just about anyone who fawns over her when she's out has an automatic free night in her bed, and though it's sad that she places so much stock in the admiration she receives from others, it appears to give her some sort of meaning or purpose. It's like she's acting out her own life as the celebrity version of herself others expect to see, instead of her true self.

"Why do you look so down? What happened? And did you know there's a big box in the stairwell outside the library?" Charlie takes a seat next to me on top of the covers of my bed.

I sigh and turn the TV off. "The box is just some documents I want to keep safe," I lie and move right along with the conversation. "As for what's wrong… Frank came in guns blazing for a good show tonight with a whole team of paranormal experts. It kind of freaked us all out to be honest, and apparently neither Sophia nor I wanted to spend the night alone after all the commotion.

Charlie bursts out laughing and then tries to hold it back when I don't crack a smile. "Oh, you're serious?"

"Dead serious." I smirk, and he seemingly tries not to smile as he visibly bites the inside of his cheeks.

"Sorry. It just sounds so ridiculous. Why on Earth would he think to do that?"

"I spoke with Grace about the things going on here, and I guess she got the impression I was concerned that Frank might be behind it all to make the show more interesting," I say with hesitation, because I never conveyed this idea to Charlie.

"What?" Charlie runs his hand through his silky dark hair as he thinks. "Do you really think he would?"

"No," I answer quickly. "I don't think so. He denied it, of course, but then he ran with the idea to play it up further for the show, even though he wasn't behind it. I just ... I don't think he would've done all that with the team of experts if he had anything to do with it."

"Well, that doesn't necessarily mean he didn't. Frank's clever like that. Always has been." Charlie purses his lips as he thinks. "So, you told Grace to sic 'em, then, huh?" He chuckles. "Boy, you really had it in for him telling her about it, didn't you?"

"Yeah, yeah, yeah. I know. Maybe I shouldn't have unleashed Grace on him just yet. Not until I had some kind of proof. She really does love to give Frank hell." I grin, thinking about how entertaining the conversation between them must've been.

"I'm sure he's done something recently to deserve her wrath anyway." Charlie laughs, takes off his shoes, and then joins me underneath the covers.

I return his laughter as he adjusts his body next to mine, only mine's nervous laughter. "Yeah, probably."

God, why did I turn the TV off earlier? That was stupid. Now there's nothing to drown out the awkward silence and nervous tension in the room.

"You aren't regretting asking me to come, are you?" Charlie asks, probably sensing my uneasiness.

"No, I just don't want to give you any expectations I can't live up to. That's all." I glance out the window where the full moon shines brightly into the room onto Charlie's face.

"No pressure from me. I'm just glad to be here, and to see you opening up again." Charlie reaches out for a reassuring hug of support.

When he holds me close to him, I can feel myself relax like I haven't in weeks just knowing he's here again to protect me. After a few seconds, he pulls away, grabs the TV remote in between us, and asks me what I'd like to watch, but as soon as he does, I grab him by the arm and pull him back to me.

Once our lips meet, he grabs me by the waist and presses me into him further, and for the first time since my accident, I feel a sensation I haven't felt in a long time—a slight tingling in my thigh despite the nerve damage. It isn't painful, it just feels odd, and it's in that moment it dawns on me that I forgot to take my medications this morning.

"Oh my God, Charlie," I gasp.

"I know." He mumbles as he continues to kiss me.

"No, not that." I smack him playfully as I pull away. "I can sort of feel my thigh again!"

Chapter 16

It's the day of the show's premiere, and to say I'm nervous would be the understatement of the century. Grace and Frank agreed, per our contract, that no publicity would be allowed or necessary from any parties related to the show. Grace and I didn't want that pressure to be put upon me on top of everything else, and I didn't want Sophia controlling the narrative out there by herself either.

So Grace concocted a public relations plan that ironically called for no public relations at all and managed to sell Frank on it because while it allows greater boundaries for me, it also prevents spoilers. There will be no interviews with any of the cast about the show until the season is complete. That way fans and the media will go crazy at the building suspense of the show.

The show will be the only avenue to us and our lives, and that's marketing genius. Her strategy gives the show another layer of intrigue and brings a sense of exclusivity to it as well. The media has already gone nuts over it, and many paparazzi have been parked outside our gate trying to get a shot of one of us filming. With this zero-promotions concept, our little show has been the most anticipated pilot of this upcoming season.

Most shows started over a month ago for the fall schedule, but we're showing up fashionably late. Sophia and I have no form of personal social media either, except for our access to the show's Facebook page, that way we're completely inaccessible. But if we all agree to it, we're allowed to go live for a quick hello on the page once the show gets going. If it's successful, that is.

"Annette, wake up." Charlie nudges me in the ribs.

Last night was the soundest sleep I've had since the accident. "What? What time is it?"

"It's five o'clock. Sophia came in at about two, so I'm going to sneak out if you're good. Your leg okay? Need any medicine?"

I hardly know what world I'm in, much less the status of my leg. I never did take my nighttime medication even though Charlie reminded me that I might wake up in a lot of pain if I didn't.

"It feels the same. The nerve damage tingling is almost gone now."

"Well, that's good. Maybe you're starting to get some feeling back. The doctors said it was possible the nerve damage was only temporary, but it could turn painful the more the feeling comes back. If it does, take the medicine and don't wait."

"I will. I will. But I kind of want to see what happens. If I don't have to be doped up on medication all the time, I definitely don't want to be."

Charlie nods before kissing me goodbye.

"Where'd you park your car?" I ask, knowing Sophia would have a fit if she saw his car in our driveway, assuming she was sober enough to even notice. I don't know what I'm going to do if she did start drinking again. She can't possibly stay here and take care of me anymore, not even for a little while.

"Old man Godfrey always said we could park over there any time we needed to avoid paps, so I did. Then I just cut through the woods."

"Aww. He's so sweet, but that's still a good walk over here from his place." I laugh, appreciating the effort Charlie put in to get here. No wonder he looked so disheveled when he arrived.

"I know. But I can always use the fresh air anyway, and you're worth it. *This* was *so* worth it." He kisses me again. "I'll call you after the premiere, okay?"

"Okay ... Hey, I love you, Charlie," I whisper after he sneaks into the hallway.

He turns around with the biggest smile as a floorboard creaks under his foot. "I love you, too, Annette."

Sophia and I agreed to watch our show premiere at home in the living room together, just the two of us. But once it's over, both of our phones are absolutely flooded with texts and phone calls. Grace is the first to call me after the show, and hers is the only call I take in front of Sophia, who's feverishly typing a text to someone with a grin on her face.

"I loved it! It's raw and realistic, even if your sister's acting her ass off. Anyone who knows her knows she isn't as nice as she came off. But it's great TV, Annette. It's going to be a massive hit!"

Getting the stamp of approval from Grace is no easy feat, and I appreciate her honesty, but if I'm a hundred percent honest, although I thought the show was great, I had a hard time seeing myself on screen looking so different. The bruises are a lot better, and good makeup can do wonders, but I can still tell I look run down and unwell despite my good efforts. I wheel into the library after Sophia answers her own phone call, so I can hear over her.

"How do you feel about it?" Grace asks.

I sigh with hesitation before answering, not really knowing how to put into words how I'm feeling without sounding vain. "I liked it, and I think it'll be great. It puts out a great message to women, but ... I can't help but feel exposed and insecure. A big part of me hates looking so, what's the word I'm looking for ... weak, maybe?"

Grace chuckles. "Annette, if there's anyone who *isn't* weak, it's you. I can sympathize with how you're feeling, but what you're putting out there is going to be great for your fans to see. It's inspiring to see how you're persevering and allowing others to witness your struggle, because we all struggle. Even famous actresses we're used to seeing picture perfect on the big screen.

I mean, it's all very relatable if you ask me, and for the record, I think you looked beautiful."

Tears well up in my eyes as she gives me the pep talk I so desperately need. The one my mom would've given me if she were here. "Right. I know. It's just ... it's hard to watch back. It really does look like someone nearly killed me."

"I know it's hard, sweetie. That's because this is all a big battle in your life right now, in real time. A real fight, not one someone wrote for you to act out. Please know how proud I am of you, and how proud your parents would be as well."

The door to the library opens, and Sophia interrupts my call with excitement. "Let's go out and celebrate! I'm meeting a friend at Saloon 5. Come on and go with me!" She motions me toward her.

Is she kidding me right now? Like a chick in a wheelchair or a recovering addict belong at Saloon 5 where people ride bulls and get trashed? "No, you go ahead. I'm actually getting really tired from all the excitement." I furrow my brows as she jingles her car keys in the air at me.

"I'll let you go, Annette. Okay? We'll talk soon."

"Alright, Grace. Thanks so much for everything! Really," I say as Sophia taps her foot on the ground.

"Are you really going to stay here all by yourself after a huge premiere like that?" Sophia has a sudden scowl on her face.

"Are you really suggesting I go to Saloon 5 in a wheelchair? Or that you go as a sober woman?"

She rolls her eyes as she walks toward the library doorway. "Fair enough, but you could have a fun time if you'd just get out of your own head a little. I'm not even drinking, by the way. I'm just going to eat and have a little fun."

"Have fun, then," I smile.

She's lying through her teeth, even to herself. Of course, she'll be drinking there, and I'm almost positive she's been drinking in my house, too. But do I really want to take on that argument with her right now and risk ending our relationship again like all the other times I tried to help her? Not really. Especially since I lack proof.

"I'll be back in time for bed. Just an hour or two, tops," she promises as I picture the couch and blankets in the living room, knowing that's where I'll be sleeping as I wait up for her.

◆

Browsing the show's Facebook page and seeing all the sympathy viewers are showing me after texting back and forth with Charlie and Monroe makes me feel grateful and awkward at the same time. The way they pour out undying support is great, but the comments about feeling sorry for me only feed my depression.

It's probably best for me to get off the page and focus on other things, though. Before the premiere, the page had eight hundred thousand likes, and now I can't help but notice that it's grown to two and a half million before I sign off.

I feel certain the ratings will soar, but I'm not quite sure how I feel about its success yet. While I wait up for Sophia, I nestle in on the couch with a cozy blanket and tell myself I'm only going to shut my burning eyes for a few seconds. I'm not asleep or awake; I'm in the meditative place between, and it's suddenly turning into the night of my accident ...

I think I hear a noise upstairs, so I make my way up there, slowly. I check all my guest bedrooms and see nothing out of the ordinary, but as I continue to inspect the bedroom closest to the stairs, the hairs on the back of my neck stand up and I get a sensation that someone was just there mere seconds before me.

Then, I flash to me writing the words *Hush, Dear Sister* on a piece of paper before I make my way out of the guest bedroom toward the bathroom. I start down the darkened hallway leading to the attic stairwell to get there, but when I reach the bathroom and take a step inside, I feel a sudden pain in the back of my head and wake up on the couch in a cold sweat.

I take a few deep breaths and wipe down my chest with my shirt, wondering if that was a dream or a memory. My pain medicine still lies on the table next to me as a reminder that I've neglected to take it all day, and though the tingling in my legs is mostly gone, my pain is definitely greater. Even so, I decide to watch a feel-good show on TV, take two ibuprofen, and doze off on the couch.

At two o'clock, I wake when Sophia stumbles in the door smelling like a bar. "My God, Sophia. You scared me half to death!" I say, trying to catch my breath after having fallen back into a deep sleep.

Sophia struggles to hang her keys by the door, and I can't believe the state she's in. "I certainly hope you didn't drive yourself home," I say before I can really think about the consequences of my accusatory words.

She turns and glares at me with pink eyes. "Excuse me. Are you suggesting I drank while I was out tonight?"

"Well, you do reek of whiskey."

"I was at a bar. Of course, I smell like whiskey. And probably a lot of other drinks, too." She rolls her eyes as she gathers and hands me all of my daily pills. "You take these already?" she asks, not completely able to make direct eye contact with me.

"No, I actually didn't take them yesterday or today, and I ..." I start to explain then think better of it.

"You *what*?" She explodes, pulling out her phone and starting to dial. "Are you crazy!?"

I wave my arms around so she'll stop dialing and look at me. "Sophia, let me finish. I think it's a good thing. I can actually feel my leg more instead of the nerve damage numbness and tingling!" I smile and wait for her reaction to my good news.

"I'm calling Spencer. This cannot be good for you. I'm not sure you should be left here on your own anymore if you can't even manage to take your medications," she says as I hear Dr. Lang's muffled voice answer the phone.

"Spencer, it's Sophia. We have a problem. Annette hasn't been taking her meds, and says she feels her leg now. This isn't good, is it?"

She then nods her head and says, "I am calm!" in a voice that is not calm at all.

"Fine. I'll tell her. Okay. Okay. Right. Yeah. Okay." She paces the room. "Okay. Thank you, Spencer. I'll tell her." She hangs up and takes a deep breath before looking at me like she's extremely disappointed.

"He said the feeling in your leg is likely a precursor to a great amount of pain if you don't take your meds. You should keep taking the pain medicine and antibiotics, that way as the feeling comes back into your leg it will return without the pain."

I tilt my head to the side, wondering if I completely believe her slurred translation. "So I'm supposed to just keep taking all this stuff even if I don't think I need it? It doesn't even hurt right now."

"Basically. Or you'll end up regretting it later when you're suddenly in a world of excruciating pain." She waves her finger at me like I'm a child who doesn't know anything. "They put a rod in your leg, Annette, and then it got infected. It's going to hurt bad. Here, take it." She tries to shove the pills directly in my mouth.

"I'll take them, Sophia, but I'm not going to be force fed!" I push her hand away as aggressively as she pushed it in my face and hold out my hand for her to give me the pills like a normal person. As she places them in my hand with force, I smell whiskey on her breath and she sighs with frustration. The potent smell makes me gag.

"You haven't even taken them yet. How can you be choking?" She rolls her eyes as she grabs her things and heads up to her room.

"I've taken them now."

She turns to look at me from the stairs as I take a swig of water.

"You can relax," I say.

She gives me a faint smile as she watches me swallow. "Good girl."

But as soon as she staggers up to her bedroom and shuts the door, I peek between my fisted fingers where the pills still reside. I turn off all the cameras downstairs with my phone and text Charlie and Monroe just as ambulance lights flash down the road toward old man Godfrey's house.

Chapter 17

Sophia eats a bowl of oatmeal very late the next morning at the kitchen table with her head hung low. I have no doubt she's hungover and feels miserable, but with the cameras on, she tries her best to look well. "How's your leg today?" she asks in a low tone.

I answer from the couch where I'm holding, but unable to read, a book with a smile on my face, "Numb again."

And I'm not lying. In the middle of the night, I had to take my medicine when I randomly started to get shooting pains up and down my thigh. It was probably just soreness from the surgery setting in, but I started to worry it would get much worse like Dr. Lang said, so out of an abundance of caution I went ahead and took them.

Disappointment that is much stronger than the pain I felt in my leg when I swallowed the pills last night fills my body, because I was so hopeful that I could go without them and have a clearer mind.

"What's the big smile for?" Sophia grimaces.

"I don't know. Good part of the book, I guess." I turn the page of the book I'm not even reading.

Sophia shrugs and takes another bite of her oatmeal and banana as I notice Monroe's car pull up at the gate outside. Sophia looks confused when the buzzer goes off, and she stands to look out the window. "What on Earth is Monroe doing here so early?"

I press the button to allow her inside just as a huge truck pulls in behind her. "What the hell? What's going on here?" Sophia raises her voice, no longer able to hide her irritation.

I place my book down on my lap with a slap and a smile. "It's a surprise."

"Oh, it looks like Charlie is with her, too. Lovely." Sophia forces a smile as she sips the last of her coffee, then places her mug in the sink so forcefully it cracks.

When Monroe and Charlie enter the front door, I greet them both with friendly hugs as Sophia looks on from the kitchen with a scowl. "What's with the big crew of men and all this equipment they're dragging out of their trucks, guys?" she asks with a look of concern.

Charlie steps forward with a confidence he hasn't shown toward Sophia in a while. "We hired a team of experts to make this place more accessible for Annette. She'll be able to connect her new wheelchair into all the new lift equipment that will be able to take her up and down all the stairs without her chair having to be moved. This way she won't need so much ... *help*," he says with a friendly tone, even though the sharpness in his eyes could cut her to the bone.

"Isn't it wonderful, Sophia? You won't have to lift me from my wheelchair to the stairlift chair anymore. And now I can use all of the sets of stairs."

"And her new wheelchair can crank up and down, so it can be her new bed rail's height for easier access!" Monroe adds with excitement as men with various tools and equipment fill the foyer with a load of supplies.

Sophia gives us all a smile for the cameras, but I can see the wheels of fear turning inside her head as she takes it all in. She's probably wondering if she won't be needed here at all anymore, and if our show will be done if that happens.

"Well, that *is* wonderful news, Annette. I'm so happy for you. Now who wants coffee?" She gives me a big hug as I furrow my brows toward Charlie and Monroe.

"Um. Sure, I'll take some," Monroe says as we all head toward the kitchen.

Sophia flipping her switch to ooey-gooey sweet wasn't exactly what any of us expected, although we did suspect she wouldn't allow herself to go completely crazy on Charlie like she wants to, not as long as she's being recorded. Maybe there's a way we can all coexist after all. Maybe she's learning to handle things with more maturity now that there's constant accountability.

Sophia turns on the tea kettle and the coffee maker, then pulls out some eggs from the refrigerator. "Anyone else up for an omelet?"

Charlie rubs my shoulders while Sophia's back is turned toward the stove, then he bends to give me a quick hug, but Sophia's eyes study him as he takes a seat across from me at the breakfast table with a huge grin on his face.

I look across the table at Charlie and wince knowing Sophia's watching him like a hawk, so I widen my eyes at Charlie then shift them toward Sophia, trying to warn him that she may be onto us. But when he finally looks over her way, he just calls her out.

"Something on my face?" he asks pointedly as Monroe and I cautiously await Sophia's response.

"Which one are you referring to, Charlie?" Sophia smiles with delight.

Charlie's smirk quickly falls into a scowl. "And what do you mean by that?"

Sophia laughs and lightheartedly throws her hands in the air. "Oh, Charlie, come on. It's just a little joke. Now tell me, guys, who wants coffee and who wants tea?"

Watching our childhood memories play out before us brings us closer together. Literally and figuratively. I guess that was the whole point of her dragging these videos out tonight in the first place.

"I remember this like it was yesterday," Sophia says with tears in her eyes as we watch our family visit to the San Diego Zoo in 1987. "Remember, that was the time the chimps started humping each other right next to the glass." She laughs, then Dad turns the camera around so we can see his face.

Seeing Mom and Dad alive and in action again makes my heart sink with a longing I can't fully process. Pictures are hard enough, but seeing them on video makes it all the more real that they're gone.

Hearing their voices, watching them move, seeing them parent us as young children—it all weighs much heavier on our broken hearts now that we live our lives without them. Sophia cuddles up next to me and takes a sip from her water bottle, which I'm starting to suspect isn't filled with water at all.

She holds me close to her and squeezes hard. "I wish they were here right now. I wish so many things had been different."

I'm feeling squished and uncomfortable on the couch with an overemotional Sophia, but I can't exactly pull away from her. She's weeping on my shoulder, and I find myself wishing I had some of her drink as I figure out how to navigate her sentiments. The video's hard to watch for me as well, but I can't help feeling sorrier for Sophia, as she must've thought this would make for a fun night of reminiscing.

I grab the remote, hit stop, and turn on *Family Feud*. "Let's take a break from all of that. It's just a little too heavy for me right now."

"Annette, I'm so sorry. You know I love you, right?" She wipes away tears on her cheeks and blows her nose into a tissue.

"I know. I know." I pull her in for a quick hug. "Now pull yourself together with a deep, cleansing breath, and let's try to have a laugh."

"Do you hate me?" Her unfocused eyes seem like they struggle to find my face even though it's right in front of her.

"Of course, I don't hate you. Do you hate me?" I laugh, and she smiles as she contemplates her answer.

"Not all the time." She giggles, and we both laugh explosively then give each other a long hug.

"Fair enough, fair enough. Hey, Soph?"

"Yeah?" She pulls her oversized sweatshirt down over her hips.

"I ... I know you're drinking again."

She stares at me in silence, so I decide to continue, "Don't you, um ... think you should get some help before things get bad like before?"

Sophia finally breaks eye contact and hangs her head low. "It's all Charlie's fault, you know."

I tilt my head to the side, not knowing what she's getting at. "What's all Charlie's fault? That you're drinking again?"

"It's funny how one day can change your whole damn life." She stares blankly at the wall behind me.

"What are you talking about, Soph?"

She continues to stare in a daze. "I was clean back then, I really was. It was a turning point for me because I really had my life together."

"Soph, that was like fifteen years ago, and Charlie had nothing to do with it." I try to rationalize it for her, but she isn't having it.

Her head whips toward me with a focused glare that could kill. "He framed me somehow. I wasn't drinking! I was the first victim to this toxic cancel culture before it even had a name ... That viral video of me getting fired for being drunk on set ruined me, Annette. It destroyed me as a person, right down to my very soul."

"But your blood alcohol level was—"

"I know what the hospital tests said ... but I *was not* drinking!" she screams, then sobs into her hands, and my eyes well up with sympathy. "And that day, it set me up for failure. A set-back I couldn't recover from no matter what I did, and I've had issues ever since. Why shouldn't I drink? In everyone else's mind I already was." She sniffs and blows her nose.

"Mom and Dad tried so hard to help me for so long ... but even they gave up on me eventually." She grabs her drink and throws it across the room with rage in her now raspy voice and I pat her on the back to calm her.

"What are you talking about? They never gave up on you, Sophia, never!"

"You don't know everything, Annette." She sobs some more. "They did give up on me."

For the life of me, I can't figure out what she's talking about, but then again Mom and Dad learned never to discuss Sophia with me after a certain number of arguments it created. Sophia didn't want me to know any of her business, and they respected that.

However, I do know one thing: even if they did have a tiff with her about her addiction, they would've come back around eventually. Dad was especially supportive of her no matter what. To a fault, actually. She always was his favorite.

"Come here." I pull her close to me, gently rock her back and forth, and start to hum *Hush, Dear Sister* ... while also wishing I'd done a lot of things differently.

Chapter 18

Sophia's still asleep in her bed, and I can't wait to see the look on her face when she realizes I got up, got ready, got myself downstairs, and made breakfast completely by myself. The way my new chair elevates me is a total game-changer. I can reach everything on the countertops now.

When I start the dishwasher, I smile with hope in my heart knowing I've turned a very important corner. And I never would've thought I could be this excited to do something as simple and mundane as running my dishwasher.

Reaching things in the cabinets is a different story, but I can always have my kitchen rearranged and modified to accommodate my needs if my nerve damage takes a while to subside or ends up being permanent. I could always have someone come and clean the house for me every day if money continues to roll in steadily, too.

Sophia emerges from her room still dressed in her robe with her hair in a messy bun. I guess she's finally starting to relax and be herself a bit more for the cameras. When she reaches the kitchen, she stops and looks at me like she's just seen a ghost, and I can tell she realizes I won't be needing her for much longer as she glances around the humming kitchen and tightens her robe with a grimace.

Suddenly aware I'm looking put together for the cameras and she isn't, she readjusts her hair into a neat bun and smooths down her wrinkled robe.

"About last night ..." she starts, and I can already tell her guard is up and she's about to change her tune about the whole drinking thing. "I don't have a drinking problem anymore. I just slipped the one time and went a little overboard. I've trained myself to be able to have a drink now and then, but last night I had a bit too much, and I'm sorry about that."

I slump further into my wheelchair with disappointment. "Soph, I don't think that's how it works. You're either completely sober, or you're not."

"Listen, I know you're concerned, but every person's individual body is different, and I know what mine can handle and what it can't," she quips, then changes the subject.

"So, let's focus on getting *you* better. I can't help you if I'm off in some unnecessary rehab facility, now can I?"

"Sophia, I don't know how much longer it's going to be necessary that I have help. I'm doing quite well now, and you're welcome to stay here, but I think maybe you need to start focusing on helping yourself." I pick at my fingernails, knowing I wouldn't be so bold with her without the cameras.

"Well, I'd like to stay a bit longer and make sure you're okay. This is only your first day being somewhat on your own, you know." She goes over to the coffee maker and starts it.

"Want some?" she asks as I check a text on my buzzing phone.

So sorry to hear about old man Godfrey next door, a text from Monroe says with a frowny face emoji.

Why? What happened? My stomach starts to knot up, knowing it must've been something horrible.

I saw an obituary posted online. It seems he had a heart attack and died at home a few nights ago. Monroe sends some screenshots from the local paper.

I cover my mouth with both hands, realizing that must have been why I saw those ambulance lights down the street the other night. The poor thing, he must have died over there all alone. God, I can't help but wonder how long he'd been lying there dead before someone finally found him.

I wake up on the couch with a puddle of drool seeping from my mouth onto the throw pillows, and I have a pounding headache. The clock on the wall in front of me says it's five o'clock, but it was morning just a few seconds ago. A blurry Sophia comes into focus and puts a blanket over me. "Are you feeling better now?" Her voice comes out in a soothing tone like my mother's.

"What? Why? What happened?" I ask, not remembering anything past her coming in the kitchen for breakfast and my text from Monroe about old man Godfrey.

"I don't know. Some kind of virus, maybe? You said you didn't feel well after you got a text from Monroe, and you kept going to the bathroom over and over like you were sick. After the fourth or fifth time, you laid down on the couch and passed out."

I bite my nails as I look around the room and fight the urge to panic at the thought of not remembering any of this. Hallucinations, voices, ghosts, gaps in my memory—maybe I *am* going crazy.

My phone buzzes on the coffee table in front of me, so I pick it up as Sophia heads toward the bathroom with a big bottle of cleaner. The phone slips from my shaky hands, and I barely catch it before it hits the hard floor.

Charlie sent a text. *Are you okay? Do you need me to come over there?*

But it doesn't make any sense. It looks like we've had an entire conversation, so I scroll up to see what I sent him.

Where's the table? I love that stream over by the bluffs, I know you know the one. All the paper here is pink.

Now I can understand why he's concerned. This nonsensical gibberish has me concerned about myself as well. The fact that I have absolutely no memory of this afternoon at all is making me feel like maybe I'm not ready to be on my own after all, and I don't even know how to begin to explain myself to Charlie.

I start to type a response, but I'm alarmed when someone opens the front door and slams it shut right beside me.

"Get out of this house, Annette," my mother turns and says to me with a pale but stern face, the one she always gave that said I'd better listen the first time or else. My hands shake, and my heart races as I rub my blurry eyes several times to make sure she's really there in front of me. But when I open them again, she's gone, and the door is standing wide open.

When I look down to text Charlie again, I see I've already seemingly written a text back ... *Get out of this house, Annette.*

As soon as I read what I wrote, I drop my phone and my whole body starts to tingle as I slowly lose consciousness.

"Annette? Can you wake up for me?" Dr. Lang's flashlight scalds my corneas.

I mumble a bunch of nothing and fidget my upper body to tell him to stop, that I hear him, and I just need him to give me a minute to fully wake up. Something else burns my nostrils as I wiggle back and forth and struggle to open my eyes, and when I finally do, I see Charlie, Sophia, and Dr. Lang all staring at me.

I push the ammonia stick in Dr. Lang's hand away and mumble again, this time with actual words. "Stop it, already. I'm awake!"

My eyes suddenly focus on the clock behind them, telling me that it's nine o'clock, but my body feels so heavy, so unlike it belongs to me.

"Annette, do you know what day it is and where you are?" Spencer asks as Charlie turns to Sophia and asks if she's sure the cameras are off.

"Of course, I do. It's a ... um ..." I try to piece everything together, but I don't know what day it is now that I really think about it, and everything seems abnormally fuzzy.

"I know I'm home," I say with slurred speech I can't control. I begin to panic at the sound of my own strange voice.

"She may have PTSD, or it could be psychosis from stress," Dr. Lang turns and whispers to Charlie and Sophia, who covers her mouth with her hands. *Psychosis? I was fine earlier today. I got down here all by myself and everything.* I try to explain that to them, but nothing comes out of my mouth.

"I think she needs to be closely monitored at all times," Dr. Lang says as Sophia nods in agreement.

I continue to lie there and stare at them, unable to lift my head. Then Charlie asks Sophia to please leave him and Dr. Lang alone with me for a minute. She looks at him with apprehension for a second, then walks off.

"Just between us, I don't know if I trust Sophia to keep an eye on Annette. I think she's been drinking again and has her own issues. Is there any way you can be around more to make sure she's getting the right medications at the right time? Or, hell,

I'll move in here and quit my job if I have to." Charlie rubs the side of his face, and I feel terrible he's this stressed.

Why can't I just get it together? Why is all of this happening to me?

Dr. Lang nods his head and touches Charlie on the shoulder with a look of sympathy. "I understand your concern, and I was actually thinking earlier that I may move in for a while and keep a close eye on things myself. I owe it to their parents for always taking care of me. This is all very strange behavior for Annette, and I want to be certain she needs extra care before I suggest her going somewhere else," Spencer explains, and Charlie sighs with relief as he digs into his back pocket for something.

"That makes me feel much better, and my offer to drop everything is still on the table if you find that you can't be here. Here's my card with all my contact info. If you could keep me informed and in the loop every day, I'd greatly appreciate it. I'll be working on set all week, but Annette means the world to me. The absolute world. And if you call me, if there's something wrong, I'll be here in an hour. No questions asked," Charlie explains as he holds back tears and pushes his hair away from his eyes.

"She's going to be okay, Charlie. This is just a setback. Perhaps she just needs an adjustment to her medications. Is there any reason to believe she's been inconsistent with them?"

Charlie looks like he's contemplating whether or not to tell him about my experiments with my meds. He eventually turns around to make sure Sophia isn't within earshot, then whispers everything he knows.

"That could be all it is. Perhaps the medication was a shock to her system when she suddenly got back on it. Or maybe she accidentally double dosed herself today," Dr. Lang suggests. "No matter. I'll get to the bottom of it and let you know."

"Thanks, Doctor." Charlie smiles, then looks at me.

"Call me Spencer, please," Dr. Lang says as they both walk toward the kitchen together. "I think she should be here alone without visitors for a few days, so I can observe her properly without her getting overly excited. I trust you'll be able to convey that to those closest to her, like Monroe?" Spencer suggests as they move further and further away from me until I can no longer hear them.

"Annette, you really need to leave this house, honey," Mom whispers in my ear at my bedside.

"Why?" I sit straight up in bed and wiggle my legs as if nothing bad ever happened to them.

"You know why." She shoots me a look of concern.

"Because something bad is going to happen?"

She nods and places a hand on my leg and smiles. I look down at her hand and go to put mine on top of hers, but then she's gone.

"Mom?" I say through my tears, heartbroken that she's gone and I can't tell her I love her. But then I'm quickly distracted from her absence when someone makes noises in the attic again, and I hear it through the vent.

I throw the covers off of my working legs and take off running until I get to the stairs leading to the attic. I open the door slowly and creep up each step as softly as I can. Someone continues to pace back and forth across the aged floorboards, and I want to see who it is just as much as I want to turn and run in the other direction. The entire attic is dark except the corner of the room the moonlight is shining in on.

Something moves toward the wardrobe, and its doors suddenly slam shut. A cold wind assaults me as I trek closer to the wardrobe. The breeze is coming toward me harder and stronger with every step I take, desperately trying to keep me from the piece of furniture that holds some sort of answer within it.

When I finally push my way to the doors, the wind comes to a halt and everything in the room is silent and still. As I slowly pry the doors open with trembling hands, I'm surprised when I find the strange box of evidence someone planted in my bathroom hidden inside.

Chapter 19

"How are you feeling this morning, Annette?" Dr. Lang brings a tray of breakfast to my bedroom and sets it on my nightstand.

I'm either too weak to answer or too tired, but I do manage to force out a small smile of appreciation.

"Good. Nice to see you're coming round a bit more. I think we need to play around with your dosages over the next few days. But don't worry, we'll get it straightened out."

He feels my head, seemingly checking for a fever. "I've got to run to the office in half an hour for supplies and an appointment, but I'll be back in a few hours," he says with a warm smile as he checks his watch. "It's nearly nine already."

"Okay," I manage to say, and he pats me on the arm.

"Good girl. Try to eat something and get some rest."

I glance over at the tray and decide oatmeal and a banana isn't worth the energy it'll take for me to grab and eat it, so I shut my eyes and fall asleep again instead.

Screaming voices wake me up, and it takes me a minute to figure out who it is.

"I want to see her myself! I heard a rumor that filming was halted because she had a mental breakdown, and I don't believe it. You better not be secretly filming her if she's struggling, or you'll regret it." Grace raises her voice at Sophia.

Sophia yells right back, "The cameras are off. See, all the lights are red, so you can relax! And you can't go in there because her doctor said no visitors."

"I want to see her myself, and I'm not leaving until I do. I trust you about as far as I can throw you, and your word means nothing." Grace stomps her feet from the foyer down the hall toward my bedroom.

"She's not in her room anyways, she's in a room upstairs now, and I told you once already to leave!" Sophia lies and calls after her, and then I hear multiple footsteps headed toward the guest bedrooms upstairs.

"I'm not going to ask you again, Grace!"

Footsteps race up the stairs until I hear grunting, moaning, and then a scream.

"Get away from me! Don't touch me!" someone says, and then I hear glass shattering followed by a loud thud. Then ... absolutely nothing.

I'm feeling weaker, and my eyes burn with exhaustion despite the terror playing out on the stairs, but I can't manage to lift my own head. The continued thud of what must be someone's body being dragged down each step makes my entire body tighten with distress, but I can't do anything except lie here and listen to the horror.

Bones hitting the hardwood floor makes my already uneasy stomach lurch, and in my gut, I know it's Grace who's being dragged, who's been hurt. Grace would never lay a hand on Sophia, even if she does despise and distrust her. But at the same time, I can't imagine that Sophia would hurt Grace either at the end of the day. Is there a chance that someone else up there attacked the two of them?

I manage to turn my head toward the hallway where my door is open halfway and see the shadow of someone dragging someone else's limp body across the foyer by the ankles. My vision is blurry, and even though I feel my heart racing in my chest, I'm unmistakably falling back to sleep no matter how hard I try to stay awake.

◈

"I'm back with lunch. I got the turkey and cheese sandwich from your favorite deli down the road." Spencer lays a new tray of food down, replacing my uneaten breakfast.

"You've got to wake up and eat a little something. You look dreadful." He lifts me up and props a pillow behind my back.

I feel myself coming to life a bit more than I did this morning, and when I fully open my eyes, I immediately panic about Grace and Sophia.

"What happened to Grace? To Sophia?" I mumble.

Spencer looks around the room as if someone named Grace might pop out of the corner. "I'm sorry, who?"

"Grace, my agent. She was here, and something broke. I think she's hurt. Can you check on her and on Sophia?" Dr. Lang feels my forehead and looks in my eyes.

"Sophia's in the kitchen, she's fine. I'll go ask her to come in here if that makes you feel better." He raises his brows then yells for Sophia.

Dr. Lang begins checking my vitals. "Open your mouth wide for me."

I gape my mouth open as Sophia enters my room looking out of breath as she clutches her chest.

"What's wrong?"

"Annette is asking about her agent, Grace. She thought she heard her here this morning. She thinks she or you may have been hurt." Dr. Lang shrugs.

"Another dream. Is that all?" Sophia sighs with relief. "I thought something was really wrong. Well, something besides all the somethings she's already got going on."

"No, Grace hasn't been here. Wait. Does this mean she's hallucinating again?" She hangs her head.

Dr. Lang shakes his head, then looks to me. "Not necessarily, probably just a vivid dream. Right, Annette? Painkillers can do that."

I feel like I must agree with him or they're both going to think I've gone mad.

"Maybe. I mean, yeah. I probably just dreamed it. I thought I heard her voice, that's all." I cover my tracks, still feeling in my gut that I didn't dream or imagine what I heard and saw. This felt different.

Sophia gives me a strange look as Dr. Lang pats me on the arm, suggesting he thinks I'm okay, and I can't help but wonder why she's lying about Grace being here and whether she accidentally killed her.

◈

After leaving a third voicemail for Grace later that night, I hang up with a horrible feeling. She's never this hard to get ahold of, and I just know what I heard was real. I shoved all my morning medicines under my pillow again today because I know something's wrong. Somebody has tampered with my meds or something, and I no longer trust anyone with my secrets anymore.

It's not that I don't trust Charlie and Monroe, I just don't trust that they'll keep quiet about the pills if something else makes me look crazy again. I mean, maybe I am crazy, and maybe this is a psychotic break or PTSD. But maybe, just maybe, it's something else. All I know is I must find out, and I must do it alone.

I check my email for something new from Grace and see nothing, so I send a quick email to her assistant to see if she's heard from her. No one can know I'm writing this, or they'll know I lied about it being a dream. Spencer abruptly enters the room wearing his coat and hat, and I jump, then realize I probably look like I've been caught doing something bad.

"I'm heading out. I have another patient to check on, but I'll be back tomorrow. Okay?"

"Of course. I'll be fine." I smile as my cheeks grow warm with guilt. Guilt for what, I don't exactly know. For lying about taking my medications, or because I no longer trust him or anyone else even though I sincerely think he's trying to help me.

Spencer hikes his bag further up on his shoulder. "Call or text if you experience anything unusual, and I'll be here."

"Will do." I fake a yawn, so I seem like I'm still on my sleep-inducing medications.

"Goodnight, Annette."

A few hours later, there's no numbness or tingling in my leg, just like before. I'm going to work through the pain this time if it kills me, because I have to figure out if I can gain back any use in it.

It sounds like a horrible idea when I say it to myself, but it's not any more horrible than feeling like I'm slowly losing my mind and independence. I watch another movie on TCM to kill time since Sophia went to bed after dinner, but my movie is interrupted by the front door gently opening and shutting.

Someone tried to keep quiet, but the squeaking of the door gave them away. Why would Sophia be going outside this time of night? Maybe she's having a drink on the front porch so I won't see her, or maybe she's sneaking out. Only I don't think she'd sneak out with Dr. Lang being gone and leave me here alone.

I decide to unmute my TV and finish my movie since I'm supposed to be doped up in here, but a few minutes later, the familiar sounds of Sophia's headboard hitting the wall upstairs drown out the film. She wasn't sneaking out, she was sneaking someone *in*.

I hit mute again, determined to find out who's up there. I turn all of the cameras back off and start a video recording on my phone. This way I know the noises I heard were in fact real, no matter what I'm told later.

It would be too loud for me to go all the way upstairs on my lift and find out firsthand who it is with my own two eyes; she'd just sneak him out the window or hide him under the bed. But if it's Frank she's sleeping with like Charlie thought, I just have to know. I check that the cameras are still off, so she won't see what I'm about to do on them later, and take a deep but shaky breath as I get in my chair.

As quietly as I can, I sneak down the hall and plant my phone behind one of the giant twin vases at the bottom of the stairs and point it up the stairs. Only I notice the vase's twin is now gone. What if that was the broken glass sound I heard when Grace was here with Sophia? I hit record on my phone and return to bed, hoping to learn something helpful from it tomorrow.

When I settle back into my bed, my leg hurts worse from all the exertion. But I can work with pain better than I can work with numbness, because at least I'm feeling something. Maybe there are physical therapy exercises I can secretly do to get a head start even though I've been warned not to. Waiting a few more weeks to try feels eternal, especially with all of the setbacks I've already endured.

I think about my camera catching Sophia's lover and smile to myself as I cover up with two extra blankets. I shut my eyes and start to drift off into a dream when I hear Sophia moan again. My mind races with questions as I bite my nails ... Who is she hiding up there? Why is it such a secret? And most of all I wonder ... What the hell really happened to Grace?

Chapter 20

"Who was here last night, Sophia?" I ask, trying not to tip my hand that I no longer trust Sophia as Dr. Lang looks over at her with a twisted mouth.

"What do you mean, who was here?" Sophia wraps her robe tightly around her like she's cold.

I give her a pointed look with confidence knowing all the cameras are on again. "Let me put it this way. Who were you having loud sex with inside your bedroom last night?"

Doctor Lang almost spits out the coffee he just took a large sip of, and Sophia's jaw drops.

"I wasn't having loud sex with anyone. I went to bed early and went to sleep. You know that." Sophia laughs and comes to pet my hair like I'm a confused child. "Are you sure you weren't hearing things again?" she says with a pout.

I turn on my phone's recording of her moaning with a man last night and play it. Unfortunately, my phone died before her visitor left her room, so it didn't capture who was in there with her. However, it *did* pick up on the undeniable sounds they made when they were together, and no one's going to tell me I just imagined it.

"I wasn't imagining *this,* now was I? Who was here?"

She looks to all of the cameras flashing green with a look of horror and knows there's no way out. "Well, not that I wanted the entire world to know, but I met a guy a few weeks ago and we got together again last night. Thanks for broadcasting it to the entire world, by the way." She covers her flushed cheeks with her hands as Dr. Lang excuses himself to the bathroom with a horrified look of secondhand embarrassment.

"Well, making me sound crazy so you can have a booty call in my house isn't exactly fair, Sophia. And frankly, I'm tired of everyone thinking I'm always imagining things."

Sophia sits at the kitchen table next to me and grabs my hand. "I'm sorry I lied about that. I just knew there were other things you heard that I didn't, and it was just easier to add one more thing to that list to keep my secret. I shouldn't have done that, though, and I'm sorry."

"Okay." I frown, not trusting a word she says anymore as she stands and rummages through the pantry for something to eat.

If she lied about this, what else has she lied about? I don't want to tip my hand too much, though, not until I've found out what really happened to Grace because Sophia will never tell me the truth. Not unless she thinks I'll be on her side.

Adrenaline soars through my body as I study Sophia digging through our selection of breakfast bars and consider the amount of danger I'm in with her here. I know I need to get out of here, out of this situation, like my mom said, but I'm in so deep now, I'm not sure how.

Do I stand by my sister if it was all a big accident, a sad misunderstanding? How could I do that to poor Grace, one of my dearest friends. Maybe Sophia just panicked after it happened and she needs some time to come clean with the whole unintended truth, but how can I trust what she tells me after I've already caught her in several other lies.

"You seem much clearer today. How are you feeling?" Dr. Lang interrupts my spiraling thoughts as he reenters the kitchen and pours himself more coffee, probably trying to change the subject.

My heart races even harder knowing I should be acting much more foggy-minded and less spry if I'm going to fool them into thinking I'm still taking my meds.

"Pretty good. I think my body has adjusted some to the medication," I lie as I clasp my shaky hands together, forcing them to be still.

"Your leg still numb and tingly?" he asks, then comes over to study it.

"Yeah. I'm hoping the nerves will heal one day when I'm used to my meds more." I force a smile, resisting the urge to wince at the ache in my leg as he puts pressure on it that I shouldn't feel.

"You okay?" He raises his brows as I try not to groan.

"Yeah, I just have a bit of a stiff back today," I lie and rub my lower back to throw him off. "I didn't sleep in the best position last night."

There's so much footage for me to review that hasn't been broadcast yet, and I don't even know where to begin. I flip through day after day of filming, trying to find a night when we may have forgotten to turn the cameras off in hopes of catching a glimpse of Sophia's nighttime visitor or any clue to her altercation with Grace.

After searching for several hours, I come up empty handed. The cameras were turned off all the nights she had a visitor, *and* they were off the morning I heard Grace. But I do stumble across some camera-testing footage during my search that shows Sophia taking my phone the day she went shopping and left me here alone. And from the looks of it, it doesn't appear she simply made a mistake.

She grabs my phone right after she put hers in her bag. And seeing it happen in real time makes it impossible for me to believe it wasn't an intentional move, even if it doesn't make sense why she would do it.

An email dings on my phone, and my notification bar says it's from Grace's assistant, Erin. I minimize the camera footage to see her response as I hold my breath with anticipation, hoping she'll say Grace is doing just fine and is back at work today like normal.

Hi, Annette, so good to hear from you. No, I haven't heard from Grace for two days...I'm starting to think I should call the police if I don't hear from her soon. Have you heard from her?

My heart sinks and my stomach churns as I read the message. I reply to Erin that she should probably go ahead and call the police just in case, and to let me know what they say. Then I call Frank. I've got to know if he or his crew has any other footage that may help me prove Grace was here.

"Footage other than what we discussed? No, I told you we don't do anything like that. You all turn the cameras off, and they're off. There are no 'secret cameras' stashed about the house that you don't know about, if that's what you're asking," Frank says with a tone of irritation.

"C'mon, Frank. I know you have something I can look at. Maybe the crew accidentally turned the cameras back on at some point. This is important. A woman's life may be at stake," I beg, and realize my voice is coming out paranoid and irrational, so I take a breath and try to calm it down.

"I promise, I won't even be mad that they did it. I just need to know who was here the other morning."

"What are you talking about? What happened over there?" Frank asks with worry. "If someone accidentally turned on a camera after you turned it off, I can guarantee you that the footage would be deleted by me immediately. But, Annette, listen, we don't hire people that do that."

I sigh with frustration, not feeling comfortable telling him whom I'm actually concerned about because, at this point, I don't fully trust anyone. What if he's the guy in question like Charlie thought? I can't let him know too much because it could get right back to Sophia.

"Whose life is at stake? Talk to me!" Frank demands, with a high pitch of desperation. "You can trust me. It'll be just between us."

"Never mind. I wish I could tell you more, but I can't. Not right now, at least."

He sighs deeply. "I wish you would. It sounds serious."

"I've got to go, Frank. I'll talk to you later. Call me if you change your mind." I hang up, knowing I've already said too much and won't be receiving anything helpful from him whether he has it or not. It's too much of a liability for him to admit it if it exists. Any secrets he's keeping are going to stay buried deep for safe keeping. Just like the one I'm still holding on to.

A new email from Grace's assistant Erin pops up on my phone, and I punch my password in incorrectly so many times I lock myself out. I scream into my pillow and wait for the time to lapse. If I can't even type my own password in because of my anxiety, then how am I going to handle what the email actually says? One minute later, I take a deep breath and unlock my phone.

Got an email from Grace today, right before I was going to report her as a missing person. She said she's taking a few weeks off because she's got the flu. She said she needs to rest and doesn't want to be bothered.

My jaw drops with disbelief because this doesn't sound like Grace at all. Erin must know that, too.

Something's off and I'm concerned. Remember a few years back when she had the flu and still showed up to my movie premiere with a mask on? She's like a machine, that woman. Believe me when I say something is wrong.

Erin writes back almost immediately, and I wonder if she's secretly glad to discuss this with someone who also knows Grace well enough to see the red flags.

I don't know what to think. She did have a bit of a sniffle last week, so it's not totally unbelievable. Maybe she finally hit a wall and needs some time off. Try not to worry for now, I'm sure she's fine. I'll let you know when I hear more from her, I promise. Knowing her, she'll probably pop in the office in a day or two when she feels a little better.

I toss my phone to the side of my bed knowing I'm on my own with this, too. If I call the police myself without Erin having my story's back, I'm only going to look crazier.

After screaming into my pillow again, I open my laptop and decide to try and focus on something else. Anything else. Because, like everything else in my life right now, I'm going to have to wait this one out.

Only as soon as I open my browser, a banner showing a new headline from *TMI* pops up showing Monroe and Charlie riding in a car together with their hands attempting to cover their faces, and it hits me like a sucker punch to the gut.

I know they're close and hang out in the same circles from time to time, but for some reason this particularly brutal headline really gets to me.

Monroe and Charlie—Inside Their Hidden Romance. A source says they're in love, but they don't want to break Annette's fragile heart.

I slam my laptop shut and begin to question everyone and everything I thought I knew. Charlie is the only one who knows the secret passageways in this house besides me. Perhaps he was more upset with me pushing him away than I thought, and he's out to get me along with Monroe?

Only Monroe has no reason to want to hurt me, and she's only ever been a good friend. Well, up until this point with all the alleged drama with Charlie, that is. Maybe they really are in love and were just trying to wait to be together until they could find a way to do it without looking like jerks. That is, until they got caught.

And what better way is there to get away with it without the public's scrutiny than to make me look crazy? It'd honestly be the best, and only, way to get away with screwing me over scot-free.

But then there's Frank ... He'd also love to make me look insane for the sake of epic ratings. As dark as it is to accept, we all inherently know that there's nothing people love more than watching a train wreck play out in slow motion.

Then there's Sophia. Her motive of jealousy seems too obvious, though, or maybe it's just simple and perfect. Maybe she's even managed to fool Dr. Lang into agreeing that I'm not all there and can't take care of myself.

So, who can I trust? No one. Except Grace. And God only knows what they did to her. What if all of this started before my accident, and I just don't remember. Maybe I found out that someone I loved and trusted betrayed me in a way that was unforgivable, and it had nothing to do with a burglary or the Red-Carpet Killer at all.

Or maybe I didn't want to go on living after I found something out, and I really did write that suicide letter. Could I have done this to myself in hopes of ending my misery? Because I'm feeling like I can relate to that in a big way right now as tears stream down my cheeks and fall onto my lap. I officially don't know what to do anymore.

Maybe I'm better off not knowing what happened that night. Maybe the pain would be too great for me to fathom and the numbness of not knowing is all that's keeping me alive right now.

I wipe tears off my face and pick up my phone to call Grace even though I know she won't answer. When it goes straight to her voicemail, I tuck myself into my bed and sob into my pillow.

But then the most unexpected thing happens, and it shocks me right out of my sorrow. Something moves at the foot of my bed underneath the sheets. *Oh, God. Please not one of those snakes they found upstairs*, I think as I muster up the courage to throw the sheets off my lower body to look. I count to three in my head as my hands reach for the covers and jerk them all up in one fell swoop.

What I find underneath the sheets is even more surprising than if there were a whole nest of snakes. There, wiggling at the bottom of my bed, is my very own injured leg and foot that I haven't been able to properly feel or move in well over a month.

This changes everything.

Chapter 21

You've been blowing both of us off ever since the TMI *article. I know you're upset, but you know us, we aren't lying to you. Please don't cut us out.*

A text dings on my phone from Monroe days later, and I shove it under my pillow where I can't see or hear it. I don't want to be tempted to let either one of them back in my life right now, not when I have a mission for the truth.

I open my laptop and notice that Sophia, Dr. Lang, Frank, and I are trending on Twitter. Our show is a massive success already, and the fact that none of us are doing any kind of promotional interviews is making it even more sought after. Everyone wants a piece of our pie like they know us, but they don't know us at all because we don't even really know each other.

I'm sure Dr. Lang will have many more celebrities seek him out for home care now that he's a household name, and he'll probably be able to drop his in-office practice completely. Sophia will find herself getting more roles now that she's redeemed herself as a clean and doting sister who was tossed aside by the previous generation. Yet I'm the one who will still be stuck in this wheelchair, allowing everyone else to benefit from my pain as I fight to get my life back to normal.

They say no publicity is bad publicity, so in that regard even Charlie and Monroe have come up off of my injuries. But there's something new none of them know about. I've been able move my leg again for days now. And as I lie here in my bed "for my afternoon nap," I'm secretly squeezing, lifting, and strengthening my atrophied leg so I can carry my weight around when everyone least expects it.

I'm still not supposed to put any weight on it or do any exercises for a few more weeks to avoid a huge setback, but doing some exercises I looked up probably won't hurt me. I've managed to stand for a few seconds at a time and bore a little weight on my leg already, and I figure with all that's been going on it might come in handy to have some tricks up my sleeve.

Hiding my nighttime pills under my pillow until the next morning has become my new normal. Then, every time I get my morning pills, I flush all of them at once and no one is the wiser. Pushing myself to the absolute limit each time I do my exercises is my biggest focus, though, because I know in my heart that someone I love put me in this position, or maybe even several who were working together. For all I know, they're also the ones who killed Vera, Diana, and Grace too, because nothing seems beyond belief. It'd be the perfect way for someone close to me to kill me, just make it look like it was a part of the serial killings.

I think about Diana and the fact that she tried to reach out to me before she died and rack my brain again about how and why I didn't get a missed call or an email from her. I've checked over my emails a million times—the trash, junk, and the archives—but there's nothing.

No voicemails or missed calls from any unknown numbers that could've been her trying to reach out either. I'm still stumped. And I guess that's what happens when you don't use social media and have a team of people to get past to be reached. She probably just didn't have time to reach out before she died.

I even checked the show's Facebook page, in case she thought of messaging me there, but I still came up empty-handed. My snail mail was a dead end as well, but I can't help wondering what other ways she might've tried to contact me. There could be something else I'm not thinking of.

I go to my Gmail again and scroll through everything once more, only this time notice something I've never seen on the sidebar. A notification on the part that says chat. I've never used that feature before, so I click it to see who the message is from, and my heart pounds as I wait for it to load. I feel like I'm going to burst open when I see that it's from Diana Rivers, and that it was sent to me the day she died. Oh, my God. This is it.

Hey, Annette. I know it's been forever since we spoke, but I'm pretty certain I saw your sister in the crowd of fans yesterday at Vera's premiere, and it made me think about how I haven't reached out to you yet. I'm so sorry to hear about your accident. I hope you know I'm praying and rooting for you even though we haven't exactly been close over the years. It's awful about Vera, too. I honestly can't believe she's gone just like that for no good reason. It really makes you think, doesn't it? Stay safe out there and take care. Let's get lunch soon.

I actually found it! She was just reaching out to show her support, not realizing what else she'd revealed in her message. I stare at the screen with my mouth gaped open as I process it all. It can't be her though, it just can't.

Sophia was at Vera's premiere, mixed in with the fans. She never said a word about being there to anyone. *What if... No. She couldn't have. Could she?* My mind spins as the realization hits me that she had the perfect opportunity and motive to kill not only Vera but Diana as well, since she saw her there at the scene of the crime.

Sophia certainly was jealous of Vera's red-hot career, and she would've had access to plant that box of evidence in my bathroom to frame me for everything she did as punishment for not being a better sister.

Footsteps coming down the stairs catch me off guard, so with quick breaths I tuck my legs under the covers and shut my laptop off. One little seed of doubt from Diana's chat message has now grown into a full-fledged forest teeming with doubts and fears in just a few seconds, and I'm feeling just as scared of my moody sister as I did when we were little.

When my puppy suffocated after getting stuck in a plastic grocery bag, I always wondered in the back of my mind if Sophia had something to do with it. She seemed almost happy about it for a split second when she told Mom and Dad the news. And she even insinuated it was my fault for not being more careful about where I left the bag even though I was certain I put it in the kitchen with the rest of them.

At the time, I convinced myself I was simply upset and reading too much into her upbeat mood despite what happened, because she'd never really bonded with the puppy enough to be sad about its death, and she *was* just a kid. But she had been pissed when she learned Mom got me a puppy, so maybe it's possible that she did do it just to punish me.

"Hey." Sophia smiles and opens the door to my room, then closes it softly behind her as she checks something on her phone. "Sorry, one minute. I want this to be off camera," she explains, then pulls her other hand out from behind her back, revealing a piece of chocolate cake.

"I feel bad we've been a little at odds with each other lately. So I baked a cake and hoped it'd be somewhat of a peace offering between us since chocolate's your favorite." She holds the plate out to me, and I'm not sure what to do.

Just looking at her, now that I know she lied about being at the premiere, gives me chills, like I'm afraid she'll be able to sense that I know. The pieces of the puzzle haven't had time to fully construct in my brain yet, but my body is already shaking as if it knows what my mind hasn't fully realized. Sophia *seems* genuine about what she's saying, but my gut is telling me to run.

She always puts on a sweet front for the rolling cameras or if she wants something from me. So when I grasp the fact that she's gone to the effort of turning off the cameras, I wonder what she might do if she thinks I'm onto her. I take the plate she offers with a smile of gratitude, cut a tiny bite, and taste it.

"Yum. So good, Soph. Thanks for doing this. I really appreciate it, but I'm really full right now." I set the rest down on the side of my bed and feel my body tremble some more.

She sits on the edge of the mattress. "Are you sweating?" She furrows her brows and cocks her head to the side as she studies me. "Here, let me fluff your pillow for you," she says, and I start to sweat even more knowing what's under it.

"No, no, no. I like it how it is, thanks. Hey, give me another bite, will you?" I say to distract her as I adjust my pillow myself, then take another bite of cake and mumble about how tired I am, hoping she'll get the hint and leave.

"Are you okay? You're acting kind of weird." Sophia leans in closer with a skeptical look on her face. "Maybe we'd better check your temperature. Hand me the thermometer."

Then as I lean toward my nightstand to grab it, she lifts my pillow from behind me and gasps. "I knew it! You've been hiding pills!" she screams and scoops them up along with my cell phone.

"Only this one time, Soph. I've been taking them later in the night when I need them, and…" I start to explain as my cheeks grow warm and my heart races, but she places her index finger over my mouth and shushes me.

"Hush, Dear Sister. No more lying."

She tucks me into bed like a wrapped-up burrito. "Sasha has taken care of it," she says in a frightening, child-like tone that makes me want to leap out of my bed and run for the hills. I start to lean forward, but a warm tingle I don't recognize is moving throughout my whole body, and I suddenly feel weak.

"You put something in that cake, didn't you? And who the hell is Sasha?" I whisper with the little bit of strength I have left, but with each passing second, I fade into a deep sleep. She poisoned Vera, cut Diana's brakes after she realized she recognized her in the crowd, tried to beat Monroe to death, and is now trying to frame me for all of it.

"No need to scream. Doctor Lang already left, so it's just us girls," Sophia says and then scratches herself on the arms and screams.

She mauls her neck and face next, then hits herself forcefully in the eye with her own fist.

"Sweet dreams," she whispers before she heads up the stairs to her bedroom with my phone and pills, screaming convincingly at the top of her lungs for the cameras that are now back on as I lie there fighting a battle I know I won't win.

FOUR DAYS LATER

The TV in my room is set to ABC, and whatever show is supposed to be playing is interrupted by a breaking news update. I open my heavy eyes to see a clip of Charlie and Monroe looking wrecked as they make a joint statement to the press.

"We firmly believe Annette Taylor is being held in her home against her will in some fashion," Monroe says, looking like she's about to cry.

"We do not trust those taking care of her and ask that someone with the power to do so help us reach her, as this may be a life-or-death situation. No one will let us visit or check on her, and we haven't heard her voice in over a week. Not to mention, one of her most trusted friends, and longtime agent who has always been her greatest advocate, has also been reported missing by her family," Charlie adds.

A member of the press pipes in, "Isn't her life being documented on film for everyone to see? She seems fine on the show."

To which Monroe replies, "The show runs a week or so behind what is actually happening in real life, and this concern is based on new developments audiences won't see play out on film for several weeks, if ever."

Another member of the press adds their two cents in, "Don't you think it's possible she just doesn't want to speak to you now that she's heard you two are an alleged secret couple?"

Charlie scowls. "All of you members of the press who have spread these vicious lies know good and well that Monroe and I have been friends for years. You also know as well as I do that you've spun this narrative of us being a secret couple into a toxic story full of false gossip that hurts real people with real lives. And no, I don't think she's not speaking to us because she believes the vitriol *you're* putting out there. I believe she's in real trouble, and that she isn't able to speak for herself right now. So here we are asking *you* for help."

The clip then fades to a different newscaster dressed in a smart purple pantsuit at a news studio who recaps the press conference. "Then, to make things even wilder, Frank Baxter, creator and director of Annette's show with her sister Sophia, chimed in with his own statement regarding Annette."

The broadcast cuts to Frank in front of a microphone making his own public statement elsewhere. "Any ridiculous drama you see between these sisters is played up for the show. Annette is fine. She's hit a rough patch in her recovery and has had to be placed in solitary confinement for the safety of herself and her loved ones. Her family asks for your respect at this difficult and private time," he concludes, which basically dismisses everything Monroe and Charlie put out there.

Frank probably received his information straight from Sophia, not knowing I've been lying here for days in and out of a forced sleep with nothing to occupy my mind but the news in front of me. *Does this mean Frank is Sophia's secret guy?*

The newscaster, who doesn't know me or anything about my life, then gives a statement from Grace Wallace's office. "And as for Annette Taylor's agent, Grace Wallace, Grace's team put out a statement several days ago saying she's been ill and is taking some time off to rest. We haven't received confirmation that she's been reported missing as of right now."

I take a bite of the bagel Sophia gave me for breakfast knowing it's probably laced with more sleeping drugs, because at the end of the day, I'd apparently rather be asleep than starve to death. After a day and a half of refusing to eat anything Sophia offered me, Dr. Lang injected me with a sedative for mine and everyone else's safety after my "vicious attack on my sister."

Sophia knows I'm at the mercy of what she says now. She officially owns me and my narrative, and I'm never getting rid of her now no matter what she's done because she's so cleverly painted this vivid picture of me being an unreliable source.

She fooled Spencer so easily with her self-inflicted wounds, and it hurts my soul and spirit to think about what he must think of me. He didn't even try to hear me out when he saw her injuries. Sophia's act worked just as handsomely as she planned for it to, and pretty soon she'll have everything that ever belonged to me ... and more.

Chapter 22

Voices in my room wake me up just enough to know someone's there. Drool slides down my cheek, and I can no longer feel either of my legs now. The silent screams in my head terrorize me as the voices around me talk about me as if I'm not here.

"Yes, she's been a danger to herself and her sister lately, so she's had to be sedated until I can figure out what's best for her going forward," Dr. Lang says calmly and rationally as Sophia cries from the corner of the room. I've got to hand it to her, she's a pretty good actress after all.

"Well, I need to ask her a few questions about Grace Wallace. She's been reported missing by her brother, and when we checked her home, she wasn't there, and neither was her car. We arrested someone we found in her vehicle who claimed they found it abandoned in a bad part of town. And when we spoke with her assistant, she mentioned Annette was concerned about Grace's well-being long before there was a reason to believe she was missing, which we found interesting," a police officer explains to Dr. Lang and Sophia as they congregate in my bedroom.

Dr. Lang sighs. "Wow. Well, I'm afraid anything she's said in the past few weeks is to be taken with a grain of salt. She's been hearing voices and seeing things that aren't there for some time now. Could be PTSD or a psychotic break, I'm not sure yet. But I'm trying to give her some time to heal before I send her out for observation elsewhere, just to be certain. So, sadly, I'm not sure you can depend on her word right now even if she was awake."

"Is the show being filmed right now?" the officer asks.

"No, no, no. I made sure it halted for the time being. The media would have a heyday with all of this, and for Annette's sake, we don't want anyone to see her in this state. Frank Baxter plans on making a statement on the show's Facebook page about it later today for the press and media," Dr. Lang explains as Sophia sniffs from the other side of the room, then blows her nose.

"Are you okay, Ms. Taylor?" the officer asks, falling prey to the attention she's seeking from him.

"Thanks for asking, but I'll be alright. I just want my sister to be okay, that's all," she says and then breaks down into tears.

"Have either of you seen or heard from Grace Wallace in the past week or two?" the officer asks as I hear a piece of paper turn over from his notepad.

"I've never met the woman myself, so no," Dr. Lang says with conviction that rings true.

Sophia clears her throat and blows her nose again. "I've not seen her in ages. I've heard her speak to my sister several times on the phone recently, but I've not seen her in person in years."

"Is it true you and Ms. Wallace have hostility toward each other because she wouldn't accept you as her client years ago?"

"Well, that's partly true, Officer. She wouldn't take me on as a client, and Grace and I were never big fans of one another for sure, but I wouldn't say we were enemies," Sophia explains with a slight tone of underlying aggression, and I can't help but wonder if the officer picks up on it.

"Do you know where your sister's cell phone is?"

"Yes, I actually have it on me right here," she says, and I imagine her offering it up to him as she bats her eyes.

The officer clears his throat. "Mind if I take a look?"

"Go right ahead, Officer," Sophia answers with a flirtatious smile I can hear.

After several minutes, Dr. Lang pipes up, "Well, if you are done with me, I need to go grab a few supplies in the kitchen for Annette."

The officer answers him, half paying attention as I envision him scrolling through my unlocked phone for clues. "Yes, go right ahead."

"Can I help you navigate that in some way?" Sophia hovers close to the officer. "Her email is down here, and her texts are over there." I'm sure she's touching him in some fashion while breathing seductively on his neck.

The officer seemingly ignores her efforts, sets my phone down on the nightstand beside me, and picks up my tray of food. "Has she not been eating? This looks like a good two meals sitting right here."

"Off and on. Sometimes she does, sometimes she throws the food at me. Depends on the day, really. She's not herself right now, Officer. These scratches and bruises are from her attacks. We're doing our best to keep her safe, though the real reason she's in this state to begin with is because she attempted suicide," she whispers, as if she's attempting to spare my reputation.

Anger fuels me as I open my eyes slightly and wiggle my tingly toes. My medication is past due, and I decide to fake sleep after I eye them and their positions in the room.

He continues to ask her questions about Grace and me, and Sophia continues to dance around the truth, only offering versions of it that make me sound unstable and irresponsible while making her shine. If only they'd leave me here alone with my phone. Then maybe, just maybe, I could escape this room and call for help.

"I was such a big fan of *The Night I Died* with her and Matthew McDaniel. It's still one of my absolute favorites. Hey, do you mind giving me a tour of the place while I'm here?" he asks Sophia, and she squeals with delight.

"Oh, of course. It'd be my pleasure, Officer. Now, the attic and basement are a hot mess right now, but I'd be glad to show you around everywhere else."

I peek just long enough to see that she has her arm locked around his as she closes the door to my room behind her. And as soon as they're down the hall, I get to work. The numbness is subsiding from both of my legs, and I need to move quickly.

I wiggle my legs as the feeling slowly returns to my knees and thighs, then I scoot myself to the edge of the bed in an upright position and wait. If I make any noise, they'll all come running and she'll convince them I'm crazy no matter what I say. So I've somehow got to manage to get myself up, into the hallway, and into the secret passageway in the library with my cell phone and some food without being heard or seen.

Part of me wonders if the officer left my phone on my nightstand intentionally; if he picked up on something being off here. Or maybe he's simply a vessel for my redemption. Either way, I'm grateful for the opportunity his being here has given me to escape.

Calling out to him with the truth of what's happened crosses my mind for half a second, but ultimately, I think I'm better off not leaving my fate up to a person who may or may not believe a word I say. It's too much of a risk with Sophia already in his ear.

I steady my legs on the floor and try to stand to my feet beside my bed, but my knees buckle, and I land back on my mattress. This is going to be harder than I thought, but given enough time unattended, I think I can do it. When I try again, I stiffen my knees more, and it works.

I'm standing as my legs shake like a newborn deer, but I'm standing. I try to soften my knees a bit as my thighs vigorously tremble, and I ultimately have to sit on the edge of the bed to rest again.

I grab my phone and stuff it down my sweatpants and underwear for safe keeping as I hold my food and two cans of unopened seltzer water. I work my way back up, take a step, then another, and then I hear the officer and Sophia in the hallway outside my bedroom door again and my palms start to sweat.

Adrenaline rushes throughout my body as I pause and stuff the waters down my underwear as well. "Well, no need to disturb her again. I've already seen her room," the officer says, and then I hear their footsteps head toward the stairs.

I reach for the doorknob and turn it with my free hand, swinging the door open quickly so it won't squeak. After stepping slowly into the hallway with a limp, I hear voices near Sophia's bedroom upstairs.

"Want a cup of coffee, Officer Brown?" Spencer yells upstairs from the kitchen as I hobble a few steps into the hallway, hoping the floorboards won't creak.

"Please, that'd be great. We're almost done with the tour," the officer answers, before suddenly realizing he's missing his iPad. "Go ahead and get that going. I'm going to run out to my car for my iPad," he says. "If you'll excuse me for just a moment, Ms. Taylor, I'll be right back."

My heart flutters, knowing my position in the hallway is visible from the front door, but it's too late to turn back now. If Sophia happens to escort him to the front door, I know I'm toast. Even if I make it into the passageway in the library, she'll know there's another exit in there when I disappear into thin air, and she'll eventually find it.

I decide to take a few steps back and wait. Officer Brown trots out to his car as Sophia's footsteps take her into the kitchen, and a few seconds later, the officer returns to join them. "Sorry about that," he says.

Now's my chance, and I'm going for it. I've never depended so much on Sophia's loud voice for anything in my life, but hopefully it'll cover the noises I'm about to make.

I shuffle my feet until I reach the library door, where my knees start to buckle as I pause to turn the knob, but I lock them up again and hold my breath as I work through the pain and force myself into the library. I keep pressing toward the fireplace. My whole body is shaking with exhaustion when I finally reach the pressure points in the molding, and I can't help but hold my breath.

I don't pause or hesitate to listen to whether the sound of the door opening alarmed anyone or not. I simply press the partially open door inward with all my strength, shuffle my way inside the passageway with a clatter as I bump into the box of evidence Sophia tried to frame me with, and shut the creaky door behind me. Then, feeling spent in every way possible, I lie down on the stone landing.

While staring up at the dusty staircase that leads all the way up to the attic, I pray. That I'll see Charlie and Monroe again and that Sophia will be exposed for the evil things I know she's done to me and so many others. Only I still can't fathom all she's done, not really, and the more I try to digest it, the more it makes my heart hurt in a thousand different ways.

Has she always been evil, and I just didn't see it? And how can I both love and despise her at the same time? I've made mistakes myself, after all—big mistakes that led me right here to this dusty stairwell.

I've held secrets of my own, lied, pushed people away I could trust, and wasted so much precious time living without the love of my life. But how am I going to be able to fix all of this? I can't protect Sophia after all she's done, as much as I want to in a way. And despite everything she's done, it hurts me to consider what will become of my sister after all of this comes out.

Chapter 23

Voices stop me from eating the bagel in my hand as I press my ear against the wall and rest my wobbly legs on the cold stone floor. The mumbling from the foyer is probably everyone gathering by the front door as Officer Brown leaves. I imagine them all saying their goodbyes as Sophia continues to play the role of devoted sister ever so convincingly, and I wish I could yell out the truth and trust that Officer Brown would believe me, because that would make all of this so much easier.

I've been failing to get a phone signal, waiting, and eating as they toured the rest of the house for about thirty minutes now, which is good, because the longer I've been missing from my bed the further I could've theoretically gotten. The last place they'll expect me to be is in a dungeon-like staircase right beneath their noses.

No doubt Sophia will assume I have an accomplice when she discovers I'm gone, and that assumption might help me learn who I can trust. As of right now, there's no way for me to know where Dr. Lang stands on this whole scheme, but I'd be lying if I said I believed him to be completely innocent at this point.

Old family friend or not, surely he's seen through Sophia's lies about me being violent. He's an educated man, and I'd think he would've put together that something seems off with her by this point.

I hear a deafening scream from my bedroom, Sophia. Then Dr. Lang races down the hallway after her. "What? What is it?"

Then ... silence. I imagine them both staring at my empty bed wondering how the hell I got out of it while blaming each other for my disappearance.

"Where is she?" Sophia finally screams at the top of her lungs with rage so deep I can practically see her red face.

Their heavy footsteps race toward the foyer, no doubt looking for me. "There's no way she could just run out of the house. The thalidomide shouldn't have worn off so quickly, unless her tolerance changed," Dr. Lang tries to explain to Sophia.

"You said that leprosy drug would keep her legs numb and tingly all the time like nerve damage! You said she wouldn't feel *anything* much less get out of bed and escape! She could be anywhere now! She could've gone to the news!" Sophia loses it with him, and then I hear a loud slap.

"Sophia! Calm the bloody hell down! She probably had someone come and pick her up is all. Call Monroe and Charlie and see if they came to get her. We can still convince them she's a danger to herself and others as long as it's me saying it. And now I have a fresh slap mark on my face we can blame on her as well, thanks to you."

"You think she's still numbed, then?" Sophia asks in a hopeful tone.

"Listen, honey. Even if she did gain some feeling back in her legs, there's no way she could suddenly get up and walk out of here. Not far, anyway. She wouldn't have the strength built up yet."

The sound of him calling Sophia *honey* makes the bit of bagel in my stomach threaten to make its way back up my throat. He's practically our uncle. How could he help her do this to me. And why?

"You call Charlie, and I'll call Monroe. Let's just see if they've heard from her for now, so don't let on that she's missing or anything. I'll say she's out with you, and you say she's out with me. Then say you're calling to ask if she's called because she was thinking of having a conversation with them both after seeing their press conference," Sophia instructs.

"That's good. We were curious if she ever did call but didn't want to ask and upset her."

A few seconds later, I hear Sophia's peppy phone voice. "Monroe, dear, I was wondering ... Have you heard from Annette today?"

Then nothing ...

"Oh, no, no. Nothing like that. She's out with Dr. Lang right now, and she'd mentioned maybe calling you to talk things out after you all went public with your concerns, but then she changed her mind. So, while she's gone, I was thinking I'd ask if she ever did call. You see, I don't want to upset her by asking, but I was hoping she'd try and work things out with you despite our differences. I also wanted to make sure you knew she was okay. It's just that she hasn't been well."

"Right. Yeah. Uh-huh. Well, I'm sorry to hear that, but I warned Charlie not to try and sneak over here several times. When the cameras caught him sneaking around the back of the house, I had no choice but to call the police, you see." Then she pauses to listen again.

"Well, do text me and let me know if you hear from her. Like I said, I'm not sure I want to upset her by asking, but I think she still needs you in her life," Sophia says before saying goodbye, and I assume Monroe is now scratching her head as she wonders what the hell that was all about.

Sophia paces the library as she waits for Spencer to return. While I listen to her fret, I can't help but piece together that she didn't attempt to call one other important person in my life that I'd naturally reach out to if I wanted to escape: Grace.

Dr. Lang comes into the library and sighs with disappointment.

Sophia immediately questions him. "Did he say anything? I don't think Monroe was lying. She hasn't heard from her."

"He hasn't, and I don't think he was lying either. She must've left on her own, somehow. She couldn't have gotten far. Let's check the house and the grounds over again. She probably got tired and just hid somewhere."

"I blame you for this, Spencer!" Sophia hisses. "If she tells everyone what we did, then I'm telling the world we started hooking up when I was only fifteen. And you better believe I have proof!"

"It was consensual!" Dr. Lang says with fear in his voice.

"I have a video, remember. Plus, I was technically a kid *and* you were a man, a married man," Sophia screams. "That's rape, *honey*."

"I've never done anything but help you with this insane plot against your sister, who I don't hate, by the way. I can't believe any of this is actually happening, that you made me do this. Just keep your wits about you and remember we're on the same team."

Sophia sniffs through audible tears of frustration. "That's not how a jury will see it if I tell the truth. So you better hope we find her."

I need to get away, much further away, but my body is frozen in fear now. God, I think I'm in shock after hearing Spencer confess his involvement in all of this. And I can't believe he was hooking up with his friends' kid when she was only fifteen. I never in a million years would've imagined they'd had an affair, or that they'd be out to get me now.

But he let her blackmail him into this. He knew I trusted him, and he tricked me into thinking I had nerve damage from the accident so she could take everything away from me and make me look insane. All while she came out looking like a doting sister on our new show that revived her career.

"You check the whole upstairs, and I'll search this floor again," she barks.

I don't trust my panicked body to be quiet any longer—the fear, hurt, shock, and panic are all trying to surface through screams and tears. But then I suddenly remember Sophia let Officer Brown know that the attic and basement were off limits during his tour, and I have to know why.

There were a lot of unexplainable things happening in the attic, and it's probably safe to assume that was Sophia and Dr. Lang working together to gaslight me. But what would she be hiding in the basement?

I fumble down the stairs toward the basement, feeling cold, distraught, and panicked as I make my way to the secret door next to the furnace. Despite the effort it took for my body to get down here, I'm still shivering with the cold chill of shock.

I manage to push the heavy door open with all the strength I have and prop it open with a brick lying on the concrete floor nearby. The only things down here are the furnace, a few shelves of paint, a broom, a wheelbarrow, two freezers, and some old bikes Charlie and I used to ride around town.

The freezers hum across the room and echo through my ears with a truth I know but don't want to face. They say you can lie to your mind but not to your body, and I know I must see it for myself to believe it even if my heaving body already knows exactly what's in there.

I shuffle my way to the other side of the room as quietly as possible while using the broom as a cane, and I find myself praying all the while that Dr. Lang and Sophia don't change their plans and come bursting into the basement.

I set the broom against the wall then grasp the handle on top of the freezer. I take a deep breath as my shaking arms tug the heavy lid up and sigh with relief when all I see is ice, old popsicles, and a few pints of ice cream. I reluctantly waddle to the freezer's sister and clutch my aching chest before I force myself to take another deep breath and lift the lid.

My weak legs wiggle back and forth with terror when the freezer's cold air hits my skin and Grace's face stares back at me. Images of frozen eyelashes and freezer-burned skin traumatize me in those few seconds, and I drop the lid then fall into a crumpled heap on the floor, unable to look at any other parts of her.

A flash of her matted blonde hair coated with frozen, congealed blood on it haunts my mind, and all of the food I've successfully gotten down comes surging back up. And even though I cover my mouth and try to keep my horrified screams in after I vomit, a desperate squeal of grief manages to escape my mouth as I try to sob in silence.

Chapter 24

I vomit inside the secret staircase by the basement after I crawl my way back in. Then I grab my phone and try for a signal, but still have no luck. If they're done searching the attic now, that's probably my best bet for getting a signal. But from here in the basement, it seems like it's lightyears away.

I struggle to stop crying but manage to shift my focus onto climbing all of the stairs in front of me with a new purpose: to not end up in the sister freezer.

When I reach the main floor outside the library's hidden door upstairs, I hear Sophia on the other side of the library walls yelling at me.

"I am so sick of your shit, Annette. Now tell me where you are!"

She screams and growls with fury as she turns the room upside down, throwing glass and knocking furniture over. "I've destroyed every camera in this house, so you might as well come out and face me, or maybe I should just turn the gas fireplace on and leave, because that's what happens when people betray me! But you deserve far worse than they did!"

I see nothing but red as it dawns on me that she's referring to our parents and their ventless fireplace that can't be left on for more than two hours at a time because it doesn't have any gas sensors. It would produce carbon monoxide if left on too long, and their detector just happened to have dead batteries when they died. *She* turned the gas fireplace back on after they went to bed, and she took the batteries out of their detector so it wouldn't wake them. My God ...

She killed our parents, too.

My eyes open and struggle to focus on the narrow, dusty staircase above me. I realize it wasn't all a bad dream and that I'm not actually in my bed all safe and warm. I must've hyperventilated and passed out when I put two and two together about my parents. Somehow, I manage to sit upright just as a wave of nausea rises into my throat again.

I bring my weak body up to my feet, hoping to go up two more floors, but realize that's only going to be possible after eating the rest of my food that still lies next to me. If I'm going to make a call for help in the attic, I need to have all the strength I can muster, but I fear that in this state, I'm probably not going to make any sense at all even if I do make it up there.

I find my phone three feet from where I woke up and thank God it didn't break during my fainting spell. No Wi-Fi, no signal. Perhaps, when I get to the attic, I'll pick something up. But first I have to give myself the best shot at survival I possibly can. I have to do this, for them.

While I force myself to eat and drink, I decide that when I get a signal, I'll first text Charlie my location and say that I'm in danger. It will require little to no explanation for him to come running. Then I'll try to phone the police if I still have time.

The shock I felt in the basement is now being replaced with rage and strength that push me onward as a surge of adrenaline flows through my body. My instinct to survive has finally kicked in.

My weak muscles feel stronger, and my head is miraculously clear as I climb the many stairs leading all the way up to the attic door while leaning on the stone rail. I haven't heard a peep from Sophia or Dr. Lang since I woke up, though, so they could be anywhere. In all likelihood, they're probably searching the grounds or hiding themselves in hopes of catching me moving to a different location.

Maybe they got into a fight and one or both of them left. Who knows? The possibilities are endless and impossible to know from my vantage point, so I need to be aware of every little noise I hear and be ready to get back in the passageway at a moment's notice, even if I don't get a chance to call for help first.

As I consider what I'll say when texting Charlie and calling the police, the thought of having to utter the words "my sister murdered my parents, my agent, and two actresses" makes me feel sick.

She's a killer. *My* sister. A real killer. I knew she had issues, but I never thought her capable of all of this.

When I press my ear to the door leading to the attic, I hesitate even though I hear nothing. No one's there, not yet anyway. So I push the door gently and pause when it makes a loud squeak.

I step forward and stop to look at my phone, hoping being one step inside is enough for a signal, but it isn't. I take a step back, go ahead and type out the text I want to send to Charlie, and press send to see if it'll work.

Message failed.

I press copy over the text and paste a new version of my message as I take a few more steps inside the attic to try again. One floorboard squeaks underneath my foot and then another. I press send again to no avail.

Copy, paste, fail, walk, repeat … until I finally reach the center of the room and it sends! My heart rate races with the relief it brings me, and for a moment, I feel hopeful. But then the door to the attic opens at the bottom of the stairs, and I panic as someone hurries up. I limp back into the secret passageway as the floorboards screech under my uneven weight, and as I try to shut the door behind me, I realize it's stuck.

I pull the door shut most of the way, but I can't latch it for the noise it'll make, so I keep a tight grip and pull it toward me with shaking arms.

"Ready or not, here I come!" Sophia sings as she scours the attic looking for me. And as she's looking around, I must assume she'll find me. Best case scenario: I'll have a few seconds to make a counterplay. But what should I do?

If I call the police, they'll just hang up or Sophia will get my phone and make me hang up. I could try to turn all the cameras on in the house, hoping she didn't actually destroy them like she said, but she'll likely get notified on her phone that they're on and turn them back off anyway.

Then something hits me like a ton of bricks—the one way I can give everyone the show they've been asking for this whole time. Facebook live on the show's Facebook page. A smile grows on my face at the thought of it, and as one of my hands continues to hold the door, the other hovers over the Facebook app's log-in page.

The wardrobe's doors slam shut across the attic, and something falls over.

"How in the hell are you doing this, Annette! I know you're up here! It's not like this house is *really* haunted. I'm sure you know by now that was me and Doctor Lang trying to make you crazier than you already are." She laughs through tears. "Well, most of the time it was us ..." she adds with a catch of fear in her voice.

"Oh. Looky what we have here! Footprints in the dust." She gasps with delight as her voice grows closer and closer to the hidden door I'm holding.

"How have I never seen this before?" She pulls the door toward her from the bottom with her fingers until it flings open despite my attempt to hold it shut.

"You're it!" She grabs and slings me forward as my exhausted legs give out beneath me, then she points her pistol at the back of my head where the safety clicks.

She continues to drag my dead weight toward the center of the room by my hair, but there's still one thing she doesn't realize. Where she can get a signal to call Dr. Lang for help, I can get a signal, too.

"Hold still, would you?" she screams, holding her phone high up in the air as I hold mine under my chest, log in, press *go live*, and wait.

"There!" she says as she releases my hair to makes her own call then presses her foot on my back so I can't move. I turn my phone face up and slide it underneath a wooden chair beside me while she looks at her phone to watch her call go through.

"Come to the attic now. I found her!" she says, relief and triumph in her voice.

I pull my arms away from the chair where my phone rests before she notices I did anything besides squirm underneath her. "I know what you did, Sophia," I say to distract her and gain the attention of everyone now listening to our live.

"Call me Sasha right now. I'm more her than Sophia. Sasha's the sister who gets things done. Don't be all shocked, Annette. You know good and well that you and your precious Charlie stole everything from me a long time ago, and I'm just taking it back," she says with a smirk, convinced she's only doing what's fair and just.

"I know I hurt you, and I'm sorry, Sophia. I know I'm not perfect. I've made so many mistakes. You're right. I wish I could start over and do things differently, but that doesn't mean you can just start killing people to get what you want in life. My God, it's bad enough that you killed Grace, Vera, and Diana, but you killed our parents, too, Soph. And now you really think you're twins like Mindy and Missy Hart. Don't you?" I throw the facts of our story out with a croaky voice I hardly recognize.

She winces. "I didn't want it to be this way, honestly, but they gave up on me. This was the only way for me to have a roof over my head again. They didn't suffer, you know. It was a gentle and kind way to go. And it made me the only family you had left to depend on when you had your *accident*."

I scream and throw a nearby textbook toward her face. "You murdered them, all of them. It wasn't gentle and it wasn't peaceful to kill innocent people and rob them of the lives they had. How do you not see that?"

"Oh, and don't forget old man Godfrey. I was talking to Sasha in the woods one night and he heard us, so ..." She winces and nonchalantly gestures with her hands that she attacked him.

"No one can hear you, you know." Sophia checks her watch, probably wondering where Spencer is. "And everyone's going to believe *you* killed Grace and company, thanks to that box of evidence with your fingerprints all over it. That and the fact that your leg was actually just fine all along."

I smile toward my phone and then look back at Sophia. "Not anymore, they won't."

Chapter 25

"Maybe I do deserve some of this because I could've tried harder to be a better sister, but Mom and Dad didn't. They never did anything but love you," I say, trying to stall for more time.

Sophia spins in a circle. "They didn't? But I think they did a little bit, Annette. They pimped me out my entire childhood and dropped me like a bad habit when I was in trouble."

"They didn't, Sophia, and you know it. They supported you and your dreams as a child, albeit Dad maybe a little too much at times, but they never *pimped you out*."

"Well, I didn't hear any complaining about the money I brought in all those years growing up that allowed Dad to quit his job. And deep down, they had to know something was going on between Spencer and me, they just didn't care."

"Sophia, I swear none of us had a clue about you and Spencer, and if they cut you off, it was after a zillion times of *not* cutting you off. They had to borrow money from me all the time because you kept sucking them dry with rehab stint after rehab stint. They probably couldn't afford you anymore!" The lump in my throat finally works its way out, and I begin to cry hysterically. The pain and longing I feel for the family we once were is gut-wrenching, and I know a huge part of all of this is my fault.

"If Charlie hadn't screwed me over that last time, I swear I wouldn't have gone back to drinking," Sophia hisses as her eyes narrow. "That was my chance, my moment of redemption, and I swear to you I was sober."

I take a deep breath and finally decide to purge myself of the terrible guilt I've carried around for way too many years. "No, Sophia, I spiked your coffee that day.

"*The Night I Died* was Charlie's big break as a writer, and we were already growing close. I'd vouched for you and instantly regretted it when you started to treat me and other members of the cast and crew terribly."

Sophia's face drops, and she stares at me like I'm a stranger. "You what?"

"I didn't want you to ruin it for everyone when you ultimately got fired for drinking, and it was too late to cut you out of the movie. I just ... I knew you'd drink again and cause a million more problems like you always do, so I just went ahead and sabotaged you at the beginning to get it over with, so they could replace you," I confess, immediately feeling bile rise in my throat.

Sophia drops the gun by her side as her shoulders droop.

"You were so vile to me in my trailer that day in front of the director, and I just snapped when you left. I don't know what happened. I guess I lost it when I grabbed your mug and poured in your favorite coffee mixed with whiskey. But it gets worse. I grabbed my purse and pulled out a few pills I'd kept from my shoulder surgery and threw them in as well."

Tears fall from Sophia's face and make bits of the dusty floor shine as she tries to speak. "You?"

"You immediately came back and gulped it down before I could take it back. It all happened so fast. And I regretted it instantly, but you left right after, and I didn't know what to do. I thought they'd fire you for appearing drunk, but I also knew Mom and Dad would come pick you up and make sure you didn't OD. But then you did! I mean, you could've died, and it would've all been my fault," I cry as Sophia still stares at me with a pallid face full of shock.

"I didn't know anyone would be filming when you got fired and kicked off the set, or that it would go viral and ruin you the way that it did. It's my fault your career fell apart back then, Sophia. Charlie never knew anything about it, honestly. And I'm so sorry I did this to you. I helped turn you into this monster."

Sophia staggers backwards until she runs right into Dr. Lang, who's now standing at the top of the stairs. "You mean, you ... All this time, you did that to me?"

Dr. Lang grabs her by the arm to steady her. "Have a seat here," he says as he pushes her down in a chair and walks toward me with a giant syringe. Sophia lays her gun down on the floor in front of her and stares at me.

"Let's not make this any worse than it already is," he whispers in my ear.

I scramble to my knees, then my feet, and make a dash for the secret door, but he grabs my arm and throws me to the ground before I make it. Knowing I've already lost, I crawl over to the middle of the room so I can be on camera as he injects me.

"Why are you doing this to me? We were friends. Please, don't do this!" I beg as he straddles and holds me down while the needle pokes my skin.

"She knows things about me, Annette. Things I don't want out."

"It was you in her bed this whole time," I cry as I wiggle away from the needle. "Somebody help me!"

Dr. Lang shakes his head back and forth and sighs. "This is just going to make you go to sleep. We don't want you fighting us the whole way to your bedroom."

"Stop. Hold on a second, Spencer," Sophia says as she walks over.

"I'm glad you told me the truth, Annette. Now you can die, and we'll both know that this was all your fault." She says then throws a note down on the ground by my face so I can read it.

"Your suicide note from the accident. Don't you remember how great I always was at forging signatures for field trips back in grade school?"

She sits down next to me to pet my hair and sings to me one last time as she cries. *Hush, Dear Sister, just close your eyes, sissy's right here, so don't you cry*, then the lights flicker and she looks around the room with a worried expression.

"Hurry up and inject her, Spencer. There really were some creepy things happening in this house, and I don't want to be up here anymore."

"Drop the needle, or I'll shoot you right in the face," Charlie suddenly says from the top of the steps with Sophia's pistol in his hands.

Spencer scoffs as Sophia digs her heels into the floor and scoots herself away while holding her hands up in the air.

"You might as well bloody shoot me. I'm going down one way or another," Spencer says, then pushes the syringe into my skin further, squeezes his eyes shut, and braces himself for impact.

A bullet smacks through Dr. Lang's chest and exits his back into the wall next to the passageway in slow motion. Spencer's limp body falls on top of me, his bullet wound gushing blood everywhere.

Sophia sprints down the stairs as Charlie leaps to throw Dr. Lang's body off of me. "Are you okay? I'm here. This is all over now," he says as he shakes my face with his hands, trying to keep me awake.

"Don't fall asleep! I don't know how much he gave you."

"They've been drugging me ever since the accident to make it seem like there was nerve damage," I whisper back to him with a smile, knowing I could always trust him.

Charlie's phone rings, and it scares us half to death when he accidentally answers it. "Monroe, it's kind of a bad time—" He suddenly stops talking and starts looking around the attic for something.

"It what? Where?" And then I figure out what she said. She must've seen the Facebook live. So I point to my phone lying under the dusty chair, and Charlie picks it up with a smile full of pride.

"Monroe says your gate's starting to be surrounded by officers, and Sophia just walked out to a small crowd at the gate. It's all on the news."

I grab my phone, turn off the live recording on Facebook, and open the news app for live coverage. Sophia's on camera, holding a black Sharpie and a stack of headshots. Walking out to the massive iron gate surrounded by news vans, fans, and police officers.

She's getting everything she ever wanted, and she takes it all in with a big smile as she twirls around in a circle, fluffing her pink tulle skirt. Sophia Taylor is officially a star again.

Three months have passed since Dr. Lang died and Sophia went viral for the second time in her life. This time it was as she was taken away in handcuffs, smiling.

Frank never would admit any to fault, but he had to suspect Sophia wasn't trustworthy when reviewing footage for the documentary and hearing from Monroe and Charlie that they believed I was being held against my will. Yet he let things go on in hopes of our shit finally hitting the fan during his beloved show. Granted, I don't think he quite knew the extent of her illness or what was going on, but our relationship will never quite be the same with the things I know he must've turned a blind eye to.

Charlie's back in my house where he belongs, and although all the things Sophia and Dr. Lang did here will haunt me for the rest of my life, I'm not allowing them to win by scaring me out of my own home.

After everyone I've lost—my parents, my agent and friend, my acting peers, my neighbor, my sister, and almost myself—I count myself grateful for whom I *do* have. There's nothing more important than *your* people, and mine have stuck by me knowing I'm by no means a perfect or completely innocent victim.

With Charlie and Monroe by my side and my ability to walk around on my own two feet again, I know there's nothing else I need. A part of me thinks Sophia's finally happy too now knowing that she's not just *famous*, but *infamous*.

As I lie down in bed with Charlie already asleep beside me, I feel a gust of cold air wash over me as goosebumps cover my skin. Even though the heat's on, I see my breath as I exhale and consider waking Charlie to see if he feels it, too, but by the time the thought crosses my mind, the ghostly draft is already gone.

Acknowledgements

First, I want to thank God for helping me see how much I truly love being an author (and for many other things as well). Storytelling is something I've always been passionate about, and now I know that writing thrillers is where I belong.

Daniel, my favorite person in the world. I can't stress enough the importance of your love and support for my writing throughout the years, and especially with this book. You're truly the best rock a person could have, and I can't thank you enough for always loving me off the ledge of my anxiety and pointing me toward the Lord.

Hudson and Graydon, you all are my heart and soul, and I love you more than any written words could ever say. I sincerely hope one day when you're old enough to read my books that you're proud of the words I've written. You two inspire me all the time, and I love you more than the universe.

To my parents and my sister, Laura, your approval and encouragement mean the world to me. I love you so much and hope you love this story just as much as the other ones. And in no way does this book describe my relationship with my amazing sister. Go read the dedication.

To my beta readers Kate, Demi, and Heather, I thank you for all your feedback and proofreading that helped shape it into what it is today.

To some sweet and supportive girl friends who need a shout-out, thanks for always being supportive from DAY ONE! Thank-you so much to Erin, Natalie, Amie, and Kaycie. You all have been above and beyond amazing to me, even before it was cool to be. Haha.

And to my fellow authors who provided the most glorious blurbs for this book, Kimberly Belle, Rea Frey, and Bradeigh Godfrey, I cannot thank you guys enough for your input, support, and kind words. I love having author friends, because you all are the best cheerleaders, and you get it.

To Sarah at Three Owls Editing, you were insightful and amazing to work with and I couldn't have done this without you.

To my amazing agent and manager, Liza Fleissig, I thank God for you all the time because you truly are the full package. I'm so appreciative of all the amazing things you do and that you are always there for me no matter what. All of us at LRA are beyond blessed to have you in our corner.

Last, but certainly not least, thank you beyond words to Kate Hergott, who helped me so much by beta reading, being my cheerleader, being my Taylor Swift twin, helped me decide on details for my cover, and supported me during the rough and happy times of this book's process. Now you can't ever leave! I truly cherish the friendship we've developed, and I trust your judgment on just about everything. THANK YOU!

To anyone who has read this book and enjoyed it, I thank you from the bottom of my heart for your love and support and ask that you write a review where you bought it before you forget. Please continue to share your love for your favorite books with your friends on social media. These kinds of things help authors much more than you know.

And, as always, a special thanks to Taylor Swift who inadvertently helps me write all my books with her inspiring words and music.

Much love,

Audra

P.S.

Go to AudraMcElyea.com and join my newsletter for an exciting announcement.

About the author

Audra McElyea is a former corporate buyer and magazine contributor turned thriller author who writes books in their villain era.

She's a self-deprecating, anxious, introvert at heart who loves her husband, little boys, and dog even more than books and movies (which is a lot).

Her taste is broad though. She loves watching Marvel and Christopher Nolan films just as much as she enjoys classic noirs like Hitchcock and Agatha Christie.

In her spare time, she enjoys reading, exercising, and listening to Taylor Swift songs over and over.

Audra is represented by Liza Royce Agency in New York.

Audra McElyea

BOOKS IN THEIR VILLAIN ERA

AudraMcElyea.com

@AudraMcElyeaAuthor on Instagram, Threads, Facebook, and TikTok

@AudraMcElyea on Twitter/X

Also by Audra McElyea

When Leighton Marx is taken at a festival in front of her loved ones, police are quick to label it a random trafficking incident, but Leighton's husband, Owen, and her ex-best-friend, Marnie, suspect there's more to the story.

After Marnie meets Sarah, who saw something at the festival that doesn't add up, she starts looking for Leighton herself—only to uncover secrets and inconsistencies surrounding her disappearance that grow deeper and more complicated by the minute.

As Marnie continues to search, she receives threats from two parties with conflicting agendas, and she must decide whether she should risk it all to find her friend, or if she thinks it'd be better for everyone if Leighton stays gone after she learns the whole, twisted truth.

IF YOU SEE ME is an edge-of-your-seat story full of unexpected turns where you can truly trust no one.

"An insidious thriller filled with scandal, drama, and oh so many twists! As we flip back and forth between past and present, McElyea gives us little glimpses of the truly terrifying world she's created. A world where no one is safe and no one can be trusted. What starts out as a simmering plot filled with unease and questions soon boils over with a twist that will make your jaw drop! Perfectly cunning and intense, IF YOU SEE ME is one you'll want to read!"
-Kiersten Modglin, million-copy bestselling author of The Arrangement

"IF YOU SEE ME hooked me from the first chapter, and the twists never stop. Told in the past and the present, with each chapter adding a new layer, it will keep you reading deep into the night."

-Samantha Downing, internationally bestselling author of My Lovely Wife

"IF YOU SEE ME is an unsettling thriller with an ominous warning: don't trust anyone, even those closest to you. Through her characters' complicated, tangled relationships in which everyone's keeping secrets, Audra McElyea drops bombshell after bombshell, creating a bingeable story filled with twisted behavior."

-Megan Collins, author of The Family Plot and Thicker Than Water

Also by Audra McElyea

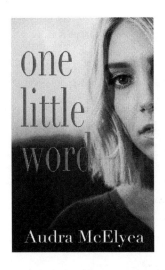

"Clever and suspenseful with characters that leap off the page, *One Little Word* creates a sense of disorientation that will keep you guessing until the very end."
- **Jeneva Rose, bestselling author of** *The Perfect Marriage*.

"One Little Word is a riveting suspense novel packed with sharp turns and unexpected twists. Single mother and widow Madeleine Barton is the perfect protagonist, capturing your heart and bringing you along for this crazy, thrilling ride. Audra McElyea is one to watch!"

- Samantha Downing, #1 internationally bestselling author of *My Lovely Wife*

"It's not easy to hit me with a twist I don't see coming, but Audra McElyea did it in *One Little Word*, a clever and compelling tale from an author to watch."

- Kimberly Belle, USA *Today* bestselling author of *The Marriage Lie*

Allegra Hudson was murdered.

An anonymous "source" drops the note into recently widowed Madeleine Barton's lap exactly when she needs it most. As a new single mother, she is struggling to make ends meet as a freelance reporter, and covering the mysterious death of local bestselling author Allegra Hudson could be the career-launching story of her dreams.

Working with Allegra's grieving husband, Connor, Madeleine plunges down the rabbit hole of the writer's privileged life. The deeper she digs, the more dirt she finds: a conniving best friend, a stalker ex-boyfriend, and a marriage in shambles. The closer Madeleine gets to the truth, the murkier the waters become.

Her source's looming presence and constant meddling in her investigation paired with her growing bond with Connor over their shared grief have blinded her to the facts, but nothing explains why Allegra Hudson's life feels so familiar. Only one thing is certain: Madeleine can trust no one.

One Little Word is a deliciously clever game of cat-and-mouse with a completely unexpected twist.

Made in the USA
Columbia, SC
20 May 2024